I0623623

MIAOW THERE!

IT'S MISTY AT SEA!

The SEAquel to All at Sea with Truffles

BY SHEILA COLLINS

FOREWORD BY ANN WIDDECOMBE

APEX PUBLISHING LTD

First published as an eBook in 2014.
First published in paperback in 2016 by

Apex Publishing Ltd

12A St. John's Road, Clacton on Sea, Essex, CO15 4BP, United Kingdom

www.apexpublishing.co.uk

British Library Cataloguing-in-Publication Data
A catalogue record for this book
is available from the British Library

ISBN: 978-1-911476-36-8

Typeset in 12.5pt Palatino Linotype

Production Manager: Chris Cowlin
Cover Designer: Hannah Blamires

AUTHOR'S NOTE

Millions of us love cruising, not least myself! My previous book on the subject ("All at Sea with Truffles") looked at cruising in a humorous way through a cat's eyes (!) when my cat, Truffles, provided us with her observations and comments. Some of you may have also read her previous Truffles' Diaries books! However, now that Truffles is up there in that big cat basket in the sky, her successor, Misty, has also decided to enlighten us with her views on one of our most popular forms of holidaying. As in Truffles' book, Misty's fictional cruise ship is a composite of two of my favourite ships and those of you who have travelled on either will recognise what she describes! I have 'combined' the two so that there is every possible facility on board for her to view! Misty has a completely different personality from Truffles so she has tended to look at different activities on board etc. Whatever, she and I hope this book will raise a smile or two!

FOREWORD BY ANN WIDDECOMBE

Alas! Truffles is with us no more but Misty is carrying on the tradition of giving us the cat's eye view. This time that view is of the seas as, inspired by the adventures of the late Truffles, Misty sets sail.

The staff are captivated and produce shrimps, the passengers smile and Misty enjoys the new experiences, walking along decks, going to shows and accompanying her PA, Sheila, to coffee shops. But she is a cat and prefers to sleep in purring bliss while Sheila goes ashore. Even the seabirds do not inspire Misty to much action.

Truffles fans will love this book and will love Misty.

www.apexpublishing.co.uk

Hello from Misty .... may I introduce myself:

Hi folks!

As my housekeeper and personal assistant, Sheila, has just said, I am now the cat in command of her house in Cornwall, U.K. I remember fat tabby Truffles from when I was a kitten and she told me all about her cruise, so since then I have always wanted to try the experience too! I was very sorry that Truffles passed on, but she is regarded as a celebrity cat author and will certainly be remembered by her human fans, so I am hoping that I will be able to follow in her famous paw prints and also be able to entertain you ... well, I will try my best anyway!

Truffles was a fat, brown striped tabby and – to be honest – quite lazy! I am small, pale grey and white and can move quite fast when I want to. Sheila's human friends describe me as "petite" and "girly" though I'm not quite sure what they mean by that! I do admit to being rather over the top by washing and grooming my fur perhaps rather too often each day, but I do like to be immaculate at all times. I had a sad start to life before Sheila took me into her home from a cat rescue centre. The people who ran it told her that I was the cleanest and fussiest little cat they had ever had in there! (not sure if that was a compliment or not!) I don't like wind and rain (either of which make me rush indoors immediately) so sometimes both Sheila and I wonder why on earth we live in Cornwall, where it appears to be windy and rainy nearly all the time! Though we did have a good summer this year thank goodness! I think Sheila wishes she could live on a cruise ship tripping around the globe to sunny places … dream on dear! And yes, though I am fussy about my appearance – well, so is she! For example, I insist that my collars are all pink to match my nose, as I must be colour coordinated. She also seems to be obsessed with colour matching her outfits and bags etc., though in her case she doesn't wear collars.

Like Truffles said in her book, cats are not allowed on cruise ships today unlike in the past where all types of ships would automatically have a cat on board to perform rodent control. This was a very good job for a cat! I do believe that nowadays, just on a few ships doing transatlantic crossings, pets can be taken on board, but they are kept separately, except perhaps authorised service dogs, and not allowed to mingle with the other passengers. So Truffles, being a celebrity cat, was honoured that the cruise line agreed for her to come on board as they knew she wanted to look at the very popular human pastime of cruising to write about in her latest book. So they allowed her to visit most places on the ship in order for her to make her catty observations and comments! Since her book came out, it seems lots of you humans have read it and smiled, so it has, hopefully, proved to be a good advertisement for cruising! So as I intend to carry on the tradition she started - of making observations on the, sometimes very strange to a cat, ways of human life - they were also happy to let me come aboard with Sheila on just one of her many trips … to Scandinavia, which I feel must be a fair distance from

Cornwall?

Anyway, let's get on with the task in hand and I will tell you all about my adventures on the cruise!

Pre-cruise Preparations:

I was feeling very excited about my forthcoming trip as I have never been anywhere on holiday except to the local cat camp when Sheila has been away cruising. It was also making me feel a little nervous to be going so far away from my safe haven here in Cornwall. It's sometimes true that home is best, they say, but it can also get a bit boring. As I said above, I am a very … I believe your human term is 'ladylike' … kind of cat. I've not had an adventurous life or been involved in sporty pursuits and rough and tumble situations. I admit I have caught the occasional slug or snail (oooh, nasty!) and one or two spiders, and once a daddy long legs, but I have never managed to catch a bird or mouse. The cats next door probably laugh at me behind their paws, but I could laugh at them now, because I would soon be doing something they certainly could never imagine … cruising!

A few days before we went, Sheila started her marathon job of packing all her outfits for the cruise. I mean, does one person really need FOUR suitcases! Her excuse, so I hear her tell her friends, is that where we live here in a country area there is just no opportunity to dress up, so all her best togs come out on a cruise ship. She also claims to never wear the same outfit twice on a cruise. Well, I guess I can understand that, because I also do not get the chance to wear many of my own wardrobe of collars! When Sheila visits stores in different countries on her travels, she always brings me home collars and treats that we cannot get around here. So we were both looking forward to swanning around showing off our best outfits!

So I sat and watched her do, what seemed to me, very hard work in bringing out umpteen different outfits and then selecting twenty eight (yes, it was a fourteen day and night cruise) plus four or five spare sets, then matching each of them with different bags and shoes, and finally deciding which sparkly ornaments to wear around her neck and on her wrists and fingers each day and evening. Phew, what a performance! It must have taken nearly all the day and at the end of it, everything she had decided on was laid out ready for packing the next day. That evening she sat doing her usual pointless activity of sitting watching a large box, while I dozed on her knee. I wondered what was ahead ...

Next morning, Sheila set to with a vengeance and by lunchtime all was neatly folded and packed except for her sparkly stuff. Of course, she paid for her ridiculous extravagance in taking so many things, because she then had to somehow get all the cases down the stairs. I smiled to myself as I watched her panting and puffing and dragging them slowly down, sometimes uttering those words that certainly cats like myself would never utter! Well dear, it's all your own fault! You could have made do with just one kittybag over your shoulder! However, once getting the cases into the downstairs hall had been accomplished, she recovered from the effort by sinking down on a comfy chair and swigging down a large cup of frothy coffee. I often wonder why she seems to love this stuff and also all those sickly smelling coloured drinks, cocktails - or cocks' tails I think Truffles called them - when she could just have water, or occasionally healthy milk, like we cats. Mind you, cock's tails do sound rather tempting as I guess they taste of chicken, and I do like a nice bit of chicken!

"Right, Misty", said Sheila, "Now it's time to do your packing!" So I sat and watched interestedly while she selected several collars, sparkly ones for evening wear and slightly plainer ones for the daytimes. I inherited a rather snazzy nautical collar that Truffles had worn on her cruise, with an anchor pendant, so I was quite looking forward to wearing that sometimes … even though it wasn't pink! Then Sheila packed the collars, my food and drink bowls, brush and comb, several bags of my cat litter, my litter tray, and one of my beds and a comfy cushion. Since I have lived with her, and after my miserable start in life which I do not wish to talk about, she has spoilt me rotten and so I have several beds, plus my own little sofa and arm chair! I often think that if we had a major disagreement, I could simply pack my own kittybag, take my furniture, move out and get my own apartment! But of course I wouldn't because I love her dearly … and I know she loves me too (Oh dear, folks, get your violins out!!) Quite recently she even bought me a day bed that looks like a boat. You can see a photo of me in it on the front cover of this book! So now I like to think I have my own little cruise ship too!

So, now all our packing was done, we could both sit back and look forward to our cruise … me with perhaps a certain amount of trepidation … Sheila with pleasure as she feels that each time she travels

on this particular ship - and she's been on it nine times in the past three years - she is welcomed back into her cruising 'family'. We spent the evening relaxing again, her idly watching the big box, me snoozing as usual, but we were each thinking "Bring it on!"

Getting Started:

Sheila came into the kitchen, where I have my bed situated under the breakfast bar, and woke me up at the ungodly hour of 6.00am ... I wondered how on earth she had managed to drag herself out of her own bed at that time - since usually she doesn't condescend to come down until about 8.00am when, no doubt, she can hear my tummy rumbling so loud that it probably acts as her alarm clock! "Come on Misty" she said, "Pop out into the garden now and be quick about it, we've got to be ready for Tony pretty soon!" I struggled to wake myself up and make sense of what she was saying ... who's Tony? What's the great rush? Grudgingly I went out through the cat flap into the garden where there was a thick dew on the grass ... not exactly encouraging me to take down my fur knickers and perform my morning ablutions! However, sensing that today was going to be something out of the ordinary all round, I thought I'd best do what she said! A few minutes later I came back to find my breakfast set out and ready for me. I must tell you that, although I sometimes - well, a lot of times really - do tend to be over critical of Sheila, she is the best possible carer (servant?) a cat could wish for, and I am so glad she rescued me those several years ago.

Whilst I tucked into my breakfast, I could hear her busy upstairs and a while later, as I washed my final whisker, she appeared again dressed in what looked like a jacket made out of a leopard's coat and toning brown trousers, all in all looking very smart. I blinked. Goodness me, this must be one of her special outfits that definitely does not see the time of day around here in this semi rural part of Cornwall. Perhaps people who travel on big luxury ships are a lot more fashionable than the people around here, I thought! Well, all to the good - because I never have a chance to wear all my fancy collars either. I began to feel anticipation brewing ... I am very conscious of my appearance, particularly my fur, and I often wish I could parade down a catwalk (excuse the pun!) modelling collars!

Then I suddenly noticed that Sheila was holding what looked like a smaller version of a dog's lead in her hand. Surely she's not going to put that on me I thought, backing away pretty smart-ish. How humiliating - dogs don't seem to mind being dragged around wherever their owners want them to go; but certainly cats decide themselves where they want to go – it's the old adage, dogs have masters, cats have servants, or to make it clearer, you people boss your dogs about – we cats boss our humans about! "Now, I'm sorry Misty" said Sheila, "I didn't show you this earlier because I knew you wouldn't be pleased, but I'm afraid that if you are coming on the ship with me, there is a condition that you must be on a lead at all times, apart from when we are in our stateroom! Ship's rules. The Captain has spoken! Truffles abided by the rules so you must too ... and I don't want any arguments!" Well, I thought to myself, she never usually speaks to me like that, what a cheek! My tail twitched. She said nothing, just held out the lead towards me. After a moment or two, I caved in ... oh well, as this was going to be an experience of a lifetime for me, I would just have to live with it. At least there would be no dogs on board laughing at me behind their paws. I walked forward and she clipped the lead onto my collar. Just in time too, because the doorbell rang - I say rang, it makes a horrendous trumpeting noise that used to scare me out of my wits when I first moved in – and Sheila said, "Oh, that must be Tony. Come on Misty."

Tony, a nice man, smartly dressed in a jacket and tie, with a cheery smile was waiting at the door and behind him I could see a large motor machine, gleaming in the early morning sun which was now getting up out of its own bed. "Hello Sheila", he said, "Well, this must be Misty. I've only ever picked her up with you from the cattery when I've brought you back from your cruise, so I've never really seen her as she's always been in a basket. Isn't she pretty!" Well, Tony, I thought, preening myself, you're my friend for life! I bet Sheila wishes that someone would call her pretty, but I'm afraid that will never happen! Sorry Sheila, dear, my first catty comment in the book – I expect there will be plenty more!

Tony looked at the line of suitcases, and also my own luggage, almost filling our large hallway, then smiled, shrugged and carried them out to the motor machine. Somehow he got them all in. "Misty's got even more luggage than Truffles had" he said to Sheila, "and I know you take enough for about four people!" She laughed, then shut and locked the front door and lifted me into the front seat of the motor machine and sat me on her lap. Well, I have to say that perhaps being on a lead was not such a bad thing because in a basket I've never been able to look out of the window and see what was happening – all you hear are rather frightening sounds that you don't understand. So, making myself comfortable, I prepared to look all around and enjoy the journey ahead – I didn't know how far away the port of Southampton was from Cornwall. It takes only ten minutes or so to get to the cat camp - this would take something over four and a half hours. To a little cat like me, an adventure in itself ...

Journey to the Port:

Well, it was quite exciting looking out of the window as we sped along the road … I could see lots of trees and once when we stopped in front of some posts with red, yellow and green lights on them, (how strange - what on earth are they? Christmas decorations?) I saw a couple of huge birds, with evil expressions, sitting on top of a tall pole that seemed to have long strings attached to it stretching away into the distance across the fields. "Buzzards, look Tony!" I heard Sheila say. Like something out of a horror film I thought – hope they never visit our garden! Fortunately we never saw any more on our journey. I was totally transfixed staring out on all sides at sights I'd never seen before …big buildings (bigger than our house!) big motor machines passing us that looked like giant houses on wheels, and by the side of the roads we drove by, more and more fields than I could ever have imagined. Lots of them contained those animals that to me look like big dogs wearing white woolly coats, and animals I did recognise that I know are called cows because they give us their lovely tasty milk! If this was just the journey to catch it, I thought, how amazing will the ship itself be! But after half an hour or so of staring non-stop at all the wonderful sights whizzing by, my eyes started to close and I dozed off.

Several hours later, I was awakened by Sheila picking me up and she decanted herself, plus me, from the motor machine.

She and Tony stretched their arms and legs, I did the same, and we all walked towards a large building that had tables and chairs set outside it on a comfy looking area of grass. They sat at one of the tables and I sat beside them on the grass and looked around expectantly. This wasn't the ship was it? Two big cups of frothy coffee were put on the table for Sheila and Tony, but nothing for me! I patted Sheila's ankle. "OK Misty, here you are" she said, leaning over and giving me some of my favourite catnip sweeties, "You're a spoilt girl!" I know, dear, I thought, and you bet I'm enjoying every minute of it!

I could hear them talking together, and it seemed that we were only about an hour or so away from Southampton. Oooh, now it really was time for me to get excited! I spent a few frantic moments titivating my fur so I would look my best when we arrived at the ship. Sheila got up and handed my lead to Tony, and went into the building saying she would only be a few minutes ... I wondered idly what she could be doing ... Meanwhile, Tony scratched me behind the ears and then began stroking my back. Nice, I thought, he has a good rhythm, I could get to like this! All too soon Sheila returned, and this time Tony disappeared into the building. What are they doing in there I wondered. Anyway, he shortly returned and once more we got into the motor machine and made ourselves comfortable. I must say I was enjoying the ride - pity Sheila doesn't have a motor machine. But I think I remember her telling someone once that if she had the money nowadays to buy a motor machine, well, she'd rather spend it on a cruise! So if she prefers to do that, well there definitely must be something in this cruising lark! Come on then, Tony, step on it

… I can't wait to see the ship!

The miles seemed to roll quickly by over the next hour and then suddenly in front of us were what seemed like hundreds and hundreds of motor machines, all pointing in the same direction as us but suddenly going so slowly that I could have easily beaten them in a race! Why had they slowed down – surely if they were all going to the ship, they would be excited too and want to get there as fast as they could? I will never understand the strange ways of you humans! "I knew it" said Tony, "it's always the same on a Saturday when there are several ships in. We'll have to resign ourselves to a bit of a wait!" I sighed, talk about so near and yet so far!

Bit by bit we inched our way towards Southampton Docks and I was totally amazed (gob smacked I believe is your human expression!) at the sight of even larger and larger buildings, and towering above them were huge metal frames that looked a bit like those things they call "pylons" that go across our fields in Cornwall (Cornwall seemed a very long way away now!) with thick chains with giant hooks on the end hanging from them. Stacks of huge wooden or metal boxes stretched as far as my (pretty sharp, I can tell you!) eyes could see. And then, all of a sudden I saw it … our ship! Like a huge mountain with rows and rows of windows. I remember Truffles telling me much the same thing had run through her mind when she'd first seen the ship. Unbelievable! It could have been all the houses in our village joined together! "At last!" said Sheila, and Tony smiled and nodded. I sat up straight and gazed all around. The motor machines were all ahead of us slowly, but slowly following each other like a herd of cows. "We're OK" said Tony, turning off to the right, "as we are just a drop off, so no queues for the car park." So we moved forward at normal speed – at last – and approached a large gateway with a small box-like building attached to it, with a man in a uniform standing in it. "Now," said Sheila, chuckling to herself, "This might be fun!"

Arrival at the port:

Tony stopped the motor machine at the side of the archway where the man in uniform was standing. Close up, he looked very fierce to me and as he peered into the motor machine, he scowled and snapped "What the devil is that?" pointing at me … how extremely rude I thought. What have I done to deserve that? People normally greet me by saying aaah, hello, aren't you pretty! And what exactly does he mean by 'that' … I am a cat for goodness sake, is he short sighted? I prepared myself to give him an almighty spit and a hiss, but felt Sheila's warning grip on my collar. "This is my cat, Misty" she replied in rather haughty tones, "and she is travelling with me on the ship." "It is definitely NOT going on that ship … or any ship" he said, shaking his fist and his face starting to turn a rather unbecoming shade of red. I was now fuming ... first he had called me a 'that' and now he was referring to me as an 'it'. My paws clenched and I inadvertently stuck a claw into Sheila's leg – whoops! Her grip on my collar tightened. "Right, calm down" she said (to him, not me) "Misty is a guest of the cruise company, and here is her passport and letter of invitation from the company. Everything is all in order as you will see." The man grabbed the documents, and after reading them, his manner changed completely. He forced a toothy smile and waved us on, muttering to himself – I have sharp ears as well as eyes – that he'd never heard anything like it and his missus would never believe it!

We drove slowly on approaching the dockside. "That went well" remarked Tony with a grin! "He was lucky I stopped Misty from hissing at him," said Sheila, "that would have put the kibosh on things, he would have blown a gasket!" They both started to laugh ... that weird sound that you people make sometimes, which to me sounds like a gang of demented chickens gabbling to each other! I, myself, didn't see anything funny in the situation, it had taken the shine off my excitement at seeing the ship for the first time, and my nose felt thoroughly put out of joint. Sheila patted me and told me not to take any notice, he was only doing his duty, even though he was pretty unpleasant about it. But it was over now, we'd passed him by and I should forget him, only good things were to come! OK I thought, she's right and I gave her a quick purr. "That's better" she said, "now here we are, so let's get out."

We had pulled up right by the side of the ship, and as I stood on the ground peering upwards - the ship seemed to go right up into the sky - it made me feel almost dizzy. Even though once or twice in my youth I have perched on some fairly high tree branches, the height of a tree was nothing compared to this. Tony bustled about unloading our suitcases and a smartly dressed man took them away, loaded them onto a trolley and then disappeared. Oh dear I thought, where's he taking them? He's got all my collars in there! Sheila must have noticed my puzzled expression for she said it was OK and the next time we saw our luggage it would be outside our stateroom door. I wondered what our stateroom would be like ... the name sounds rather royal to me ... sounds posher than cabin. No doubt I would find out later! After thanking Tony for a very pleasant journey, Sheila took a firm hold of my lead, grasped her handbag and with her pulling along a slightly smaller suitcase on wheels, we walked along the dockside until we came to some glass entrance doors leading into what seemed like an enormous building crammed full of people all talking at once and most of them carrying or pulling an assortment of similar suitcases or bags. I instinctively moved closer to Sheila's leg. I was thankful for the lead again, because attached to her, I knew I'd be safe. "It's OK, Misty" she said, "don't be scared. If Truffles could do this, so can you – everyone will love you, don't worry!" We approached a smiley lady, again smartly dressed, and as Sheila showed her our documents, the lady told us that she had been looking out for us, and they were delighted to have us on board. How nice, I thought, and gave her one of my pussy smiles. She leaned down and patted me, "What lovely fur" she said. I preened myself, things were definitely looking up! Straight ahead and turn left to Elite Members' Check In she told us. She stuck a sticky label onto Sheila's jacket. What's that for I wondered … why didn't she put one on me … but then I noticed that stickers of different colours were put onto everybody's coat. Must be to keep track of everyone I thought, and I noticed that all the people wearing blue stickers went to queue at one desk, the reds to another and so on. Our sticker was gold and we didn't have to queue!

We strolled across in the direction she had indicated, surprising quite a lot of our fellow passengers who seemed to be doing a 'double take' when they saw me! Don't know why … havn't they ever seen a cat before? I heard a few comments like "Have I had a few, is that a cat I saw?" and "That can't be a cat, can it?" and "Is that the ship's cat?" I smiled to myself, I was going to enjoy all this! I remember Truffles telling me that she also had revelled in all the attention.

We arrived at the desk marked "Elite Check In" and there was another very smartly dressed, smiley lady there to greet us.

Checking in and getting on board:

On the other side of the desk was yet another smartly dressed lady in nautical style clothes ... my collar would have added the finishing touch I thought ... and she gave us a beaming smile of welcome. How very different from that awful fierce faced man at the port gates! "Hello and welcome" she said, "I've been asked to look out for you! We've all been saying how unusual it is to have a cat sailing with us – though I do seem to remember we had one last year." "That was Truffles" laughed Sheila, "yes, it's the cat lady here again!" They both laughed. Sheila passed over our documents and the lady tapped away on some hidden machine. All seemed to be in order. She then gave Sheila a form to fill in to confirm we had not been ill or suffering from colds, tummy bugs or whatever. This cruise company is one of the best in the world and exceptionally keen on health and safety, taking great pride in having everything spotless and gleaming on the ship, so Sheila tells me. It's one of the many reasons that she chooses to cruise with them. And I, too, wouldn't settle for anything less!

I pride myself on being healthy ... I have all the annual vaccinations and, naturally, Sheila gives me regular pedicures, flea drops and ear and eye checks etc. I eat only the best food (not own brands!) and keep myself spotless. It pays off... touch wood (an expression you seem to use, though I don't really see the point of it) I don't mix with the neighbourhood cats as, firstly, they are a bullying bunch and much larger than me, and we have crossed paths in the past, and also I don't want to pick up nasty feline diseases or, heaven forbid, ticks. Not sure why I have digressed on to this rather depressing subject ... sorry, too much information! So to continue ...

Next, the lady said she was going to take our photos. Great, I love having my photo taken! Sheila doesn't, though, because she's not as pretty as I am (Ouch! Sorry Sheila!) She always says that ever since she started writing books, she's had her picture put in all sorts of magazines and papers etc. so she wishes she was a bit more glamorous! Photos completed, Sheila was handed our Sea Pass and then the lady wished us a happy trip and we left the desk. Soon we had to join another queue (When were we ever going to actually get to the ship, I wondered impatiently!) of passengers waiting in front of yet another archway with a stern faced official standing beside. Next to him was what looked to me like a tunnel and into this people were putting their small bags and cases. These then disappeared into the tunnel whilst their owners walked through the archway. Sometimes this archway made a beeping noise, and then the official held out a strange looking object – looking rather like a black hairbrush to me – and passed it around their bodies and this strange object also made squeaking noises. Now these sounds, to me, were quite pleasant reminding me of those furry little delicacies with long tails! When it came to our turn, I held back, my tail twitching. I didn't want to be picked up and put into that strange tunnel.

Fortunately I wasn't. Whilst Sheila put her bags into the tunnel and walked through the archway, the official, who now didn't look so stern faced - in fact he actually seemed to be laughing - held on to my lead. He even leaned down and patted me. "Well, well madam" he said to Sheila, "this is a first for me! A cat going on a cruise! Ha! Ha!" All seemed in order, so no squeaks for us as we went through ... pity!

Holding on to my lead again, Sheila trundled her suitcase along with me trotting by her side and we threaded our way through the crowds of other passengers until we arrived at something that looked rather scary to me. I drew back again. It was a staircase, sort of similar to ours at home, but it was, it definitely was ... it was moving! However, Sheila turned to the left and then we approached something that looked even more scary. It looked like a cave but it had doors in front of it that slid from side to side. I saw people going through these doors which immediately closed. A few minute later they opened and the people came out, but they looked different! How could that be? I'm not going through those doors I thought, I might come out looking like a dog! "Come on Misty, don't be a scaredy cat! This is called an elevator and will take us for a ride up to the next floor" Sheila said. Oh well, if you're sure then, I thought... so with me keeping as close to her as possible, we got in. And to my relief, when we got out a few moments later I still looked the same, but we were now on a different floor and the moving staircase had disappeared. This was certainly a day of revelations for me , and we still had not even got on to the ship!

But, we were nearly there now. We walked towards another passageway and I saw that there were two young men holding cameras and taking pictures of passengers as they approached. More photos I thought! Wonderful! I gave my chest fur a quick lick. We stopped and Sheila, I noticed, had drawn her tummy in and put on her best smile ... well, I think she would have said that the young men were very nice looking so maybe she wanted to make an impression? The young men seemed quite surprised to see me, I can't imagine why, but Sheila picked me up and held me in her arms and so they took the photo. Then yet another long passageway loomed ahead sloping upwards and so we started walking again. The passage zigzagged to and fro and we seemed to be for ever climbing but not getting very far. Sheila was puffing a bit but that was her own fault, as (a) she doesn't take enough exercise, and (b) she shouldn't have put so much heavy stuff into her suitcase! Thankfully, we eventually came to the end of the passageway. What a tedious way to climb I thought. This route could only have been designed by a human, certainly not by a feline specialist, who would have simply made it a straight vertical quick and easy climb! But at last we stepped on board! Yippee!

Sheila handed our Sea Pass to another smartly dressed and smiling man, who put it into a slot in a machine which then pinged, sounding rather like the chirp of a bird. Nice, I thought, mouse squeaks and now birdsong ... just as if everyone knew they were having a cat visitor! Next, we passed another nice looking young man (no wonder Sheila likes cruising so much if she's surrounded by handsome young men!) and he squirted something on to Sheila's hands. Not sure what it was as he didn't put any on my paws. Sheila put down her bags and rubbed her hands together. "Well, Misty," she said, "I'm glad to stop for a moment after dragging that heavy case along. I really shouldn't bring so much!" Huh, when she gets back from her cruises with yet even more stuff than she started with, she's always saying she shouldn't take so much. Well, learn dear, learn!

Next, we ambled along to where a line of ladies, all smiling ... I have ever seen so many smiling people before, how nice it was ... were welcoming the passengers with a drink of that bubbly liquid you all seem to like. Sheila took her glass and walked over to a nearby area with comfy looking armchairs, and sat down with me by her feet. "Well, Misty, here we are. Welcome on board, your adventure is about to begin!" She raised her glass, "Here's to you!" Not quite sure what that expression means, but there you go ... I looked all around me at the crowds of people that had followed us on to the ship and these people, I noticed, were looking at me too! I preened myself. Again I heard comments like .. is that a cat? Can that possibly be a cat? How many glasses of this stuff have I had dear, I thought I saw a cat ... etc. etc. Oooh, this was going to be fun I thought. I could get used to being the centre of attention; I remember Truffles telling me that she enjoyed being thought of as a 'celebrity cat' too.

We sat there for a while, Sheila accepting another glass of bubbly from yet another nice looking young man. As many other passengers passed us by, doing the usual double take when they saw me, if I heard her say it once, I heard it a hundred times ... Yes, hi, good to meet you. Yes, this IS a real cat! Yes, she IS pretty isn't she. Yes, she is a special visitor. We're writing a book about cruising.

"Now then, Misty" said Sheila a little while later, "It's a nuisance, but I can't go and have lunch as I usually do because you are with me, so I think we'll have a wander round until the staterooms are ready at about 1.30 and see if any of my friends among the crew are on board." I briefly wondered why she couldn't have her lunch just because I was with her, it's certainly never stopped her before when we're at home. We hadn't gone more than a few paces when all of a sudden a guy with a beaming smile rushed up and gave Sheila a big hug! I looked up at him in amazement. I know that for some odd reason, human men seem to shave off their face fur, but this guy had shaved off the fur from the top of his head as well! He looked like a smiley pumpkin! His head was so shiny, you could see your reflection in it I guessed … that is, if you were rather taller than I am! Actually, I was to see many other men with shaved heads later during the cruise. It is obviously very trendy, so I guessed he could be described as 'a pretty cool guy'! No cat would ever, ever want to get rid of its fur (unless it was one of the rather unique Sphynx breed) A cat's fur is its best asset! When you are choosing us for your pets, the colour and length of our fur is an important consideration, and we also choose our mates for their appearance too, so quality and colour of fur means a lot to we cats!

"Well, well," he said to Sheila," I didn't know you would be on this trip so soon after your last one, great to see you again!" They grinned at each other, looking like two Cheshire cats! "Well, good to see you too Michael" she replied. She introduced me and he bent down and tickled me behind the ears and stroked my back. I switched to purr mode. Oh yes, I

thought, you are a nice man, I know we will be friends. " Well"
he said to me,"I've heard all about you Misty! I have Truffles'
book from when she was on the ship and I believe you are
going to let us all have your observations as well." I nodded
and stepped up the purr a notch. Sheila then told me that
Michael was the Activities Director on board so no doubt we
would be meeting up a lot and there would be many things for
me to look at with all the activities and entertainment they have
on board which Truffles, being rather lazy as I've mentioned
before, didn't want to join in. I sat down again while they
chatted away catching up on what had happened since she was
on the ship about three months earlier. I idly wondered to
myself whether when Michael was out in the sunshine, it
would reflect off his head or, if he was out at night, would the
stars reflect on him too? Maybe if we get to know each other
better, he might let me sit on his shoulder and use his head as
a looking glass, I do like preening myself ... Then Michael said
he had to go, so he walked away in one direction and we
continued on our way and sat down for a further half hour in
another nice sitting area, Sheila chatting to some people nearby,
all of us waiting until it was announced that the staterooms
were ready.

Arriving at our stateroom:

Shortly afterwards, I heard a lady's voice that seemed to come from above, saying that our rooms were ready. I looked all around, but I couldn't see the owner of the mysterious voice. So many things were baffling me already about this ship, I had the feeling that this cruise was really going to be an eye opener! With Sheila firmly gripping my lead and pulling along her suitcase, we strolled along until we arrived in front of several of those elevator machines, something like the one we had seen in the port. These, however, were all made of that weird material you call glass which, I have to admit, is just something that we cats, and dogs too, find so very hard to understand. You can see right through it but you can't walk through it. Unbelievable! Unlike the rather dingy and dull one we'd been in earlier, these elevators were gleaming with highly polished surrounds starting right at the ground, so I could very easily look at myself (!) and the doors slid back silently and all in all, it looked most inviting. Now that I had had the experience of riding in one of these contraptions, I wasn't at all nervous and so I bounded in ahead of Sheila, giving a few people that were already standing inside something of a shock. Out came Sheila with the explanations again! The doors closed and then again I heard a mysterious lady's voice saying "Deck 7 - doors opening" Again I looked all around me but could not see the owner of the voice. Weird, weird! "Doors closing" she said and off we travelled again. When she said "Deck 10", Sheila said, "That's ours, come on Misty" and so we got out. Beyond us I could see a big room filled with rows and rows of books. There were several more of those comfy chairs set out with small tables handily placed nearby. Now, because of Truffles and her books, I do know what a book is though I don't know how to read one myself! But I had never seen so many all in one place. Sheila keeps quite a few in her study at home on a few shelves, but this was something else. "This is called a library" Sheila told me. Well, you learn something every day!

Leaving the 'library' area, beyond us stretched a long passageway with lots of doors each side of it. We have, I've always thought, lots of doors in our house, but here simply everything I had seen so far was just so very much bigger! A lot to take in for a little cat like me, but I was sure that after the initial day or two, I would soon find my paws! After walking along a lovely soft carpet, bliss to my said paws, and passing two or three of these doors, Sheila stopped at one, marked number 1122, and said to me "Here we are Misty – welcome to your new home for the next two weeks!" She reached into her pocket (I remember Truffles telling me that she always wished she had had a pocket - very handy for carrying dead mice or spiders around!) took out our Sea Pass card, and slid it into the door where it made another satisfying chirping sound. Then she opened the door and behold (!) I was looking at a stateroom!

Around our stateroom:

Sheila led the way, the door silently shutting behind us. Unclipping my lead, she disappeared into a door leading off directly to the right, so whilst I had a few minutes to myself, I had a good look around the stateroom. It was larger than I had imagined – somehow I thought it was going to be a pretty compact compartment with a view, rather like my room at cat camp. But then I thought, silly me, she couldn't fit all that luggage into anything small, could she! Carrying on past the door on the right, I came to a large clothes cupboard (closet to our American readers) ... a wardrobe I think you call such things, but why a cupboard would want to go to war – and who against – I have no idea. Next to that was a very large and extremely comfy looking bed with lots of soft pillows and cushions on it and to each side was a baby table and shelves. On top of one of these was one of those high tech gadgets you speak into. I never have understood exactly what these things are. We have several at home and Sheila also seems to carry a tiny one in her bag. For some reason she speaks to them from time to time ..... aaah, perhaps they get lonely! Above the splendid bed were more cupboards attached somehow to the wall.

I carried on my exploration, and a little further on was a beautiful pale leather sofa. That's more like it I thought, I expect she'll put my favourite furry cushion on that so I can relax in total comfort. I am never allowed to get on her bed at home so I guessed there was no chance of her changing the rules here either! I was dreaming of some blissful sleepy moments on the sofa when suddenly I jumped nearly out of my skin! Unheard by me, Sheila had opened the mysterious door and there came from beyond it a very frightening sound the likes of which I had never heard before! I shrank back underneath the bed! What the ..... was that?

"Misty" she said, "now, there is something you will have to get used to hearing whilst we are on the ship, so I want to show you so you won't be scared." Too late, I muttered to myself, I AM scared. And no, I am NOT coming anywhere near it! I retreated further under the bed, but her arm reached under the bed and pulled me out ... "It's OK, Misty" she said, picking me up and patting me, "It's just the sound of the loo. I won't get technical with you, but all ships have very noisy loo's. It's so the water can flush instantly away and just as instantly, refill. It's nothing to be scared of, really. I'm going to take you to watch as I do it once more to show you that it won't harm you ...that is," she smiled to herself" as long as you don't try to jump into it!" No chance of that, dear, I am definitely going to keep my distance! Why don't ships have nice quiet litter trays for their guests instead of these noisy water boxes! At home, yes, she has three of these loo's (water boxes I call them) but they don't seem to make any noise – she is the only one that makes the noises! (Oh dear, another catty comment Sheila!) She carried me into the little room; I could see that it was a nice bathroom now. We approached the loo and, still carrying me, she leant towards it saying, "just watch, Misty, nothing nasty is going to happen to you, but you just must get used to the noise!" I cringed back against her but did force myself to look closely. She pressed a button and sure enough a torrent of water shot downwards making the loud noise that had startled me so. But as she had promised, it was over in a moment and no, now I had seen it, it wasn't in the least scary! Oh, well, what a anti climax! I jumped down and as she went on into the main stateroom, I looked closely around the bathroom.

Not sure why it's called a bathroom as it didn't have a bath in it! It had one of those overhead pipes that spouts water spray over you … personally I couldn't imagine anything more loathsome than having water sprayed over me, ugh! Still, each to their own I guess. There was also a lot of drawers and shelves and a tall side cupboard with a glass (that mysterious stuff of which there seemed to be so much on this ship) front, and there was also a large looking glass with lights over it. Well, Sheila would enjoy preening herself in here I thought! Investigations complete, I came out into the stateroom again.

Opposite to the bed and sofa I could see a range of units containing more drawers and another small cupboard, inside which, when Sheila opened it, I could see it contained lots of little bottles of those coloured liquids that you all like, some of which make you giggly if you have too many! Above that was a smaller cupboard door, but I don't know what was behind that! Fixed to the wall above the units was one of those flat square box like things that shows pictures that Sheila seems hypnotised by each evening at home, though it wasn't quite so big as ours! Aha, I thought, I've found just one thing that on this ship is not as big as the ones we have at home! And finally at the end of the room on this side was a desk type unit with a chair in front and another looking glass above. On this desk were some nice flowers and one of those things I think you call a kettle where you make your frothy coffee and stuff. In the centre of the room just in front of the sofa was a low table on which were more flowers and also a big bottle of that bubbly stuff that Sheila likes, with some drinking glasses beside it. Beside that were several booklets and what looked like small newspapers. Well, I thought, we'll certainly be comfortable in here!

"Just one more thing for you to explore, Misty" said Sheila, "and that's the balcony." Balcony, what's a balcony? She edged me towards some of those glass sliding doors at the far end of the stateroom. We have something similar in our house and that's where I like to sit and enjoy the sunshine - when we get any that is! Sheila slid the doors open and we walked through. Something else that was very strange ... outside our doors at home there is green grass, here it was just a wood floor and I could see above me a table and there were two very long chairs plus paw rests. (not sure what you call them!) At the end of this wood floor there was what l looked like another glass wall but it only reached about halfway up Sheila. "Come and look, Misty" she said. I walked gingerly up to the glass wall, and looked through it only to jump back with a start! OMG, no grass to be seen but just water, water as far as the eye could see! Reminded me of a nightmare I had once when I dreamt I fell into huge pond and couldn't get out! After my nerves had calmed down a little, I crept forward - very slowly indeed - and peered out again. In fact, now I could see that there were some of those large buildings in the distance so I supposed that it wouldn't be too bad to be surrounded by water if I could see land in the distance. I breathed a sigh of relief and looked up at Sheila. "Of course, we're only in the port at the moment," she said,"Once we start moving, you will see what a big sea is really like, but don't worry, you'll soon get your sea paws!" She walked back inside and left me sitting there puzzling. What on earth was she talking about … C a big C! C paws! Was she talking in some kind of code? I shook my head. Oh well, although I am pretty quick and understand most of what you humans say, there are times when I think you talk out of the backs of your heads … and this was certainly one of them! I sat there for a few minutes in the sunshine thinking this would be a pretty nice place to relax. Suddenly there came a bang at the stateroom door and Sheila opened it to see a nice looking dark haired young man, smiling at her … and he had all our luggage. My first thought was thank goodness, my collars!

"My goodness, it's Pedro!" she said, "how nice to see you again." "And you too Mees Shella", he replied in a rather strange accent that I didn't recognise. Certainly not Cornish and not really like how Sheila speaks either. "Well, I knew I was having the same stateroom as I had on my last cruise" said Sheila, "but I didn't realise you would still be here too! How are you?" "Fine" he said, "I just have this cruise to do and then I will be going on leave myself." He pushed all the cases inside, and after a few minutes chatting, Sheila picked me up and introduced me to him. He patted my head and said "Ello Mistee, you are a prettee pussee, I 'av been told to expect you, and I will be your personal steward for this cruise !" They both laughed. Oh, I was enjoying all this! I switched on my purr at full volume and he said that anything I wanted, I only had to ask! Well, as I said earlier … the saying that cats have servants was now definitely proving to be true! Sheila has always said that the service on this cruise line is the best, and I was already beginning to believe it! Time would tell! After a few more moments of chat, Pedro left and Sheila turned and surveyed the cases. "Well, Misty" she said, I'll get you sorted out first and then you can go and sit on the balcony while I unpack all my things before we have to go to lifeboat drill." What's that I wondered.

She unpacked my bed and placed it in a corner by the glass doors, then put my comfy cushion just outside the glass doors so I went and curled up on it deciding to have a quick catnap after all the excitement of the day! When I awoke about an hour later, I could see that my litter igloo had also been placed outside in the opposite inner corner of the balcony. That's handy I thought, I'll use that right away! Sheila then came and quickly did her litter cleaning and changing duty, decanting the used litter into some special bags she had brought. The elf and safety people on this ship are, apparently, very fussy and exacting on anything to do with hygiene,and I knew she would do everything just as required. I believe she had agreed all this with them when she was planning this trip. Well, I do have her very well trained in these duties at home in any case, so I would expect no less than first class service from her at any time, wherever we might be! I followed her back inside the stateroom and all the cases had now disappeared and everything looked neat and tidy. I know that Sheila is very fussy and back at home everything must be just so and in its proper place. Luckily I feel the same, so that's another reason we get on so well! She leant down and clipped the lead onto my collar once more and told me we were now going to the mysterious lifeboat drill. Well, all would soon be revealed and it would be yet another new experience for me on this exciting day!

Lifeboat drill and leaving port:

We walked along the passageway to where the elevators were, but this time just as I was about to pull forward in their direction, Sheila turned instead to the bank of stairs nearby. I noticed that some other people were using them rather than the elevators for some reason, and there were more smiley members of the ship's staff all dressed in - rather unbecoming I thought - yellow waistcoats, waving everybody towards the stairs. I wondered why? Oh, maybe the lady who announced the different floor

numbers had a sore throat and couldn't speak, so was having a rest perhaps? We were on deck ten so we made our way down to deck five, Sheila as usual acknowledging the comments people were making about me. It was beginning to get a bit wearing now I thought. I'm a cat, I'm here, it's all above board (excuse the pun!) so get over it!

After getting to deck five, Sheila gave our stateroom number to a man with a long list and he smiled and patted me saying that he had been told to look out for a cat passenger and he was honoured to meet me! How nice – I gave him a purr. We strolled over to some nearby chairs and Sheila sat on one with me sitting underneath. I felt safe and more or less unseen in this hiding place, and I could have a good look around too! Apart from lots of peoples' legs walking by, I could see there were many tables and chairs in this very large – dining room I think it is called - and above I could see lots of sparkly lights hanging from the ceiling. It all looked very attractive and the tables were set with those things you eat and drink with – glasses, lots of them, and various hand tools. We cats have no need of such things, two simple bowls – one for food and one for water – and our mouths and paws are quite sufficient. Don't know why you don't follow our example; think of all the hours of washing up you'd save!

After a short while I felt Sheila, who had been chatting to the people nearby, take hold of my collar and mutter to herself "Wait for it". "Wait for what?" I thought. A rather loud unseen man's voice was talking to everyone in general …I could'nt help but wonder where all these invisible people were, first the lady in the elevators and now this guy somewhere above! Suddenly I heard seven short, but very loud, hooting sounds followed by the same thing but this time very long and drawn out … horrific! I wanted to stick my paws in my ears, but unfortunately I can't get them into that position! You humans can, I know! It's perhaps one of the few things I envy about you as it would be useful from time to time, and this was definitely one of those times! I shrank back further under the chair, but Sheila told me to calm down, and that everything was OK. She said this was a sound we hoped we would never hear again (believe you me, I certainly agreed with her!) and it would only ever be used if we had to get into the lifeboats. These, she explained, are hanging on the outside of the ship but we don't want to ever get into them! I pondered to myself – what a waste of time if we don't ever want to get in them, why do they put them there in the first place? I repeat, I will never understand the strange things you humans do! Anyway, after a bit more talking from the unseen man, followed by the man - who had taken our names before - putting on and then taking off again (what an odd thing to do!) a smaller orange jacket - that suited him even less than the yellow one - everyone got up and made their way back towards the stairs. So that was lifeboat drill was it? Oh well .....

After climbing from deck five up to deck ten, Sheila was puffing and panting! I, on the other paw, wasn't out of breath at all. You definitely need to take more exercise, dear... As we walked back towards our stateroom I was fascinated by rows of sparkly little green lights that had appeared by the side of the passageway. They hadn't been there when we left earlier. How pretty. It wasn't Christmas was it? As we passed the lights I had a bit of fun patting several of them but they didn't go out. We arrived at our door and immediately Sheila sat down on the leather sofa and put me on her knee. "We'll be leaving very soon, Misty" she said, "so I'm going to drink a toast as we leave". What on earth is she going on about now, I thought. How can you drink toast!

After Sheila's puffing had ceased, she picked up the bottle of bubbly stuff that had been on the table and, wrapping its top in one of those fluffy rags I had noticed in the bathroom that wasn't a bathroom, she then spent about five minutes twisting it about trying to get its top off. What a performance I thought – it seems much easier to open a milk carton! Eventually with a sound rather like a damp firework (one of those frightening things to we cats!) the top of the bottle shot out and bounced off the wall. I fielded it neatly and had a pleasant few minutes knocking it around the stateroom floor whilst Sheila busied herself wiping up the splashes from the table and filling her glass. "Come on Misty" she said, "we're about to leave now." She walked over to the glass door leading to the balcony and I followed, a trifle nervously. Once outside she sat down on one of the long seats and I sat looking through the glass wall. All of a sudden a very loud hoot, that made me jump, came from the ship and I could see that very slowly we seemed to be moving! The sun glimmered and shimmered on the water below, making me feel quite light headed for a few moments until I became accustomed to it, but after a while it felt very relaxing. I could hear the sound of people's voices that seemed to be coming from above and also music. Everyone certainly seemed to be very happy! And so was I … We both sat there for about half an hour or so watching the port of Southampton disappearing behind us, and I was also fascinated by all the seagulls that were temptingly flying past us. We get a few of these noisy birds at home but nothing like so many as were around us here. "Now" said Sheila, "it's nearly time for your dinner, Misty, so I'll give it to you now but after today I'll be able to order whatever food and treats you want from room service and Pedro will bring it for you." Sounds good I thought. I found that I was feeling pretty hungry after all the excitement of the day, so when she put down a dish of sliced turkey in gravy (and not an 'own brand' tin either!) I wolfed it right down. Feeling full and comfortable, I curled up on my comfy cushion, now moved inside, and very shortly slipped into sleep mode, only waking when Sheila, now wearing a much dressier outfit, came and patted me, saying she was going for her own dinner now. Leaving the glass door open a bit so I could reach the litter igloo if required, off she went. Sleep overcame me once more!

The first evening on board:

I was suddenly awakened by a knock and the noise of the stateroom door opening. I leapt off the cushion and ran under the bed. Peeping out I could see two legs walk past and a voice said "Ello Mistee – where are you?" I breathed a sigh of relief, it was OK, I recognised Pedro's strange accent, the likes of which I had never heard before in Cornwall. I came out of my hiding place and he patted me. I rubbed myself round his ankles and switched to purr mode. I was going to make sure I kept in his good books (one of your quaint human expressions I believe) so that he'd give me lots of lovely treats! I rearranged myself on my cushion again watching him as he walked around the stateroom turning down the covers and removing the fancy cushions from the top of Sheila's bed, propping them up on the back the sofa. Handy, I thought, I'll try them out for comfort later! I heard the sound of water flowing and him moving things about in the non bathroom, and finally he came out with one of the fluffy white rags and deftly folded it into what looked like a turtle, leaving it on top of the bed together with a couple of chocolates ..... I know that Sheila spends a lot of time eating chocolates so I knew she'd definitely be pleased to find these when she got back!

"Well Mistee" said Pedro smiling, "what 'av I got for you 'ere I wonder!" He felt in his pocket (Oh I wish I had a handy pocket!) and produced two lovely fat pink shrimps! Wow! I swiftly got off the cushion, switching up the purr a notch, and sat looking up at him expectantly. He dropped them at my feet, gave me a final pat, said he'd see me tomorrow and disappeared out of the door. Well, I could get used to this lifestyle! If this was what cruising was like, I could well see why Sheila enjoys it so much – all the pampering! Something I have to admit that I get from her at home, but I know she doesn't really get any! I savoured the shrimps for several seconds before they slid deliciously down my throat, and then after cleaning my whiskers I jumped up on the bed to investigate the fluffy white turtle. Mmmmm, it felt very nice so I flexed my claws on it for three minutes or so. Somehow at the end of this soothing exercise the turtle looked rather ragged but I hoped that Sheila wouldn't notice. Next, I investigated the cushions on the sofa but being rather shiny and slippery, they didn't, in fact, feel as cosy as my own furry cushion. So, after popping out to the litter igloo outside, I returned to my cosy corner and dozed off again, dreaming of shrimps, turkey and all manner of other goodies which I fully intended to sample over the next two weeks.

I have no idea when Sheila came back but I was awoken by her smoothing the top of my head and telling me to get up as we were going for a walk around. She had enjoyed her dinner and had some nice people sitting at her table. She had also been somewhere called the Martini Bar and had had a couple of nice cocktails there. Cocks' tails? Mmmm, they sounded rather appetising to me, I love chicken! Following a leisurely all over stretch and a pleasant scratch, after my rejuvenating sleep I felt up to anything so I watched and waited whilst she disappeared into the non bathroom again, when I heard the horrendous flushing water sound that I supposed I would get used to after a few more days. Coming out she preened herself in front of the looking glass and added some more of that shiny pink stuff she puts on her lips. Ugh, definitely something I wouldn't fancy on my lips, but then, they are pink enough already and my collars usually tone nicely with them and my nose too! However, on this occasion I saw Sheila pick out a very snazzy silver, not pink, sparkly collar - that I'd never seen before - from my bag, and as she put it on me she told me that we would both be 'dressing up' in the evenings. Well I am all for that, no chance to do that where we live in Cornwall! So, matching sparkly lead clipped on, off we went …

We strolled along the passageway and I saw that the pretty little green lights were not lit up any more. Pity, I thought they looked nice. We arrived at the elevators and there were several other people chatting and waiting there. As we approached them, a bit of a silence fell and I preened myself and acknowledged their smiles and surprised expressions. Sheila again explained how come she had a cat with her! This was beginning to get a bit tedious I thought, but hopefully once people got used to seeing me around the ship, they wouldn't look so surprised … but I have to say, I did rather like being the centre of attention! We got into one of the elevators, and once again I couldn't see where the mysterious lady who announced the deck levels was hiding! At any rate, Sheila and I got out at deck number four. I enjoyed the ride and looking out of the glass walls of the elevator I could see a large REAL tree hanging in mid-air in a large pot as we passed swiftly downwards. Baffling! All the trees at home stick out of the ground, they don't float in the air! Another sight to remember!

Then the sights and sounds became really exciting and confusing for me! Leaving the elevator, Sheila led me towards what looked like a bridge made of glass bricks - and coloured lights showed through it. "Come on Misty" said Sheila, "we're going to walk over this bridge and then ahead there is the shopping street where I must try not to be too tempted!" She laughed to herself. Well dear, I thought, I know that you can shop for England so your friends all say, but they won't tempt me because I don't have any money! I can never understand you humans and your money ... most of you seem to moan that you havn't got any, and then when you DO get some, you go and give it all away to the shops! The shopkeepers must be rubbing their paws with glee! We approached the glass bridge and I shrank a bit closer to Sheila's leg as it looked a little scary and slippery. Once we were on it, though, I realised it wasn't frightening at all and a novel experience to be able to see underneath where you were walking. I looked down and could see more people walking on the deck below and there was nice catchy mewsic coming from some jolly looking men wearing big hats in what Sheila pointed out to me was a Salsa Bar. Arriving at the end of the bridge, we started to wander along the street. People looked at us, needless to say, but all their comments were nice and all sorts of people patted me ... I felt like a film star!

The first shop we passed was one of those frothy coffee places she likes - I guessed she'd be visiting that tomorrow! Next to that was a general store selling all sorts of stuff like chocolates (oh dear, Sheila!) and bottles of those coloured sickly drinks you like, and after that there were lots of shops selling those sparkly things you wear round your necks and on your arms and paws, those little bags you carry in all different shapes and colours (oh Sheila, you told a fib when you said you hoped you wouldn't be tempted ... dream on!) and everything else you could think of. I noticed a shop selling little teddy bears. I sighed, she'd definitely be buying one or two more to add to her collection at home that I have to live with. She brings them back from all her travels. I sometimes think we have a private bear zoo at home. We next came to one of those drinking places where you like to meet up (pubs I think you call them) called The Dog and Badger. My goodness me, I hoped there weren't any dogs and badgers about. I pressed even closer to Sheila's leg as we passed here! Then glancing across to the other side of the road, I had an even bigger shock! Parked outside another little drinking and snacking place was a bright blue painted motor machine! Surely these didn't drive around on ships! But it wasn't going anywhere I soon realised as it wasn't making the roaring noise that I suppose makes it move - it seemed to be just there for show and, I blinked, two giant teddy bears were sitting in it! People were taking pictures of the bears in the motor machine and everyone was laughing! Before I realised what was happening, Sheila picked me up, sat me on one of the bears and took my photo too! Roars of laughter from the people around us!

Reaching the end of the street, we started down the opposite side and really there was so much that I just couldn't take it all in. My head was whirling with everything I had seen during today, more than I could ever imagine or had ever seen in my entire life! We passed another place selling drinks and things that Sheila called pizzas ... heaven alone knows what they were! Next was a shop that seemed full of little bottles and boxes. A sickly sweet smell hung in the air – ugh! Sheila stopped here and steered me in through the doorway. She picked up two or three of the little bottles and sniffed them appreciatively telling the assistant she'd probably be in there tomorrow to buy some. I sincerely hoped she wouldn't bring me with her as the overpowering sweet smells were making me feel quite nauseous!

Not soon enough for me, we left the shop and I gulped in some fresh air. Ooh, that felt good! I felt Sheila quickening her pace, "Mustn't be too long here, Misty" she said, " as it's nearly time for the show.

What's a 'show'? I wondered. Carrying on we next passed a shop that seemed to be filled with those little time telling machines that you humans wear on your paws. We don't need such things. I can tell the time in three different ways: by the sun, by the moon and by my tummy! After the time shop we came across a much more useful place, I thought, selling ice creams. I rather like the odd lick of an ice cream, particularly chocolate flavour, though I wish some cat loving human would invent mouse flavoured ice cream! I saw that this shop, Sheila called it an ice cream parlour, was called Ben and Jerry's. Should have been Tom and Jerry's shouldn't it? We were nearly at the end of the street now and next was one of those places where you male humans have your face fur and head fur cut off. Stupid habit. Finally we passed by a shop selling clothes you wear to do sports and outdoor pursuits. I noticed Sheila never even glanced through its window ...well, as she thinks the only form of exercise she needs is walking around inside shops, I could see how it wouldn't appeal! We were now back at the glass bridge again, and I have to admit that it was hard trying to get my head around all that I had seen on this ship. I was buzzing, really I was! My life has been confined to one house and one garden, plus a few sorties into the neighbours' gardens – this ship was a whole new world. And now we were going to a 'show' ... what was that going to be? Up we went in the elevator to deck five, and no I still couldn't see the lady who told us when we got there! After what seemed quite a long walk, we came to the theatre, where Sheila said the 'show' would be held. I wondered what would happen next ...

"Now Misty" Sheila said, "you're very lucky that I am taking you into the theatre. I'm pretty sure that no cat has ever been in here before - except perhaps Puss in Boots" (she laughed to herself) What on earth was she talking about now, I wondered, she does drift off at times! Anyway, in we went and she sat down on a high chair in front of a wide ledge, rather like a bar in one of those pubs I mentioned earlier, and sat me on the ledge. Looking around me and downwards I could see rows and rows of seats ... wherever I looked there were seats and more seats! People were coming in and gradually filling up all these seats. Everyone was sitting looking towards what looked to me like a large square bit of floor (I learnt later it is known as a stage) with long curtains behind. To be honest, it didn't look particularly exciting. Rather puzzled, I looked up at Sheila who smiled and said "In a minute you will hear some lovely music and there will be people singing and dancing, and all sorts of nice things to watch. You know you like listening to music, Misty!" Well, yes I have to say I do like your mewsic, better - to be honest - than our local cats' chorus which meets on our neighbour's wall every Friday night. "And", she continued, "We have a special treat tonight because a good friend of mine, Peng Fei, who comes from China, is going to perform and he does all sorts of wonderful things on the stage, but tonight he is doing his famous face changing show." Well this really "purrplexed" me! I stared up at her in amazement. Firstly, I assume that if Peng Fei is from china, he must have to take great care of himself in case he breaks. And, secondly, how can he change his face? However, Sheila was busily looking around the theatre, so I kept pondering. A few minutes later another unseen voice from above told people they must switch off their phones (those irritating little boxes that you are for ever speaking into) and that they mustn't take flash photos, they mustn't do this and they mustn't do that and that the show would start in a few minutes. Sheila smiled. "That's Michael's voice" she said. "keeping us all in order!" Come to think of it, the voice did sound vaguely familiar, yes it was the smiley man we had met when we first came on board. Suddenly the lights got dimmer and dimmer until there were none except those shining on the stage. Of course, with my cat's eyes, although it was dark I could still see all the people in the seats quite clearly … so anybody who gets up to any mischief, watch out, Misty's about!

The curtains opened and a burst of mewsic came from a large group of humans holding all manner of instruments. A band I think you call them. It was wonderful! The mewsic I enjoy comes out of a box at home, but this was amazing and something you could really watch. I sat up eager not to miss anything. After the mewsic ended, everybody clapped their paws together and a lady dressed in a very colourful yellow and green outfit came on to the stage. She was wearing the highest heeled yellow paw covers (sorry, you call them shoes!) I have ever seen. I reckon I could have crawled underneath them! "That's Sue the Cruise Director" whispered Sheila," she has the most wonderful shoes!" Well dear, I thought, wishful thinking in your case - you'd never be able to walk in them! Sue was welcoming everyone and telling them about things that were going to be happening on the ship … too much for me to bother even trying to understand … and then she waved her arm and a troupe of very glamorous young girls came on with some hunky young men and they all sang and danced around while the band played. At the end everyone was clapping and whistling. Next Sue brought a man on and he was speaking to everyone but every few seconds people were laughing at him. Poor soul. He must have felt awful. I don't know what he was talking about but they obviously thought it was funny. How embarrassing for him. Still, at the end of it he seemed cheerful enough! Finally Sue came on and announced Sheila's friend Peng Fei. How was he going to change his face I wondered!

The band was now hidden behind the curtains and some other rather strange sounding mewsic started up. After a moment or two I got used to the unusual soulful twanging sounds and it became rather soothing to listen to. All of a sudden a person appeared dressed in flowing robes and with a strange mask like headdress. He twirled here and there, waved his arms and legs about and then swiftly turned around and, wow, his head looked totally different. I blinked. My eyes are very sharp, but I did NOT see the change! This happened at least another eight or nine times. I felt totally Misty-fied (excuse the pun!) and it was really wonderful to watch. At the end, the young man's real face was finally uncovered and all the people clapped very loudly and many of them stood up. "Well", said Sheila, "I feel so proud of Peng Fei. He is amazing and, Misty, he does a lot more things than face changing which you will see later, and I am honoured to be his friend." She picked me up off the ledge and we joined the crowd of people leaving the theatre.

Walking along deck five we came across another frothy coffee lounge, rather more elegant than the one on the shopping street below, and Sheila sat down at a table, with me underneath it. From my hidey hole under the table I could see several people sat around drinking all manner of coffee and chocolate drinks and even the stuff that I know Sheila is not keen on herself, tea. I also noticed that at the far end was another ice cream place, though this was called a Gelateria. Sounds rather posh I thought … I'm definitely going to get Sheila to let me sample some of that!

We sat there for a short while and then a nice looking girl, who had been walking around giving drinks to people, approached us with a big smile! "Oh, hello Violetta!" said Sheila, "how good to see you again, how are you?" They hugged each other. "It's a latte with Amoretto, isn't it?" said Violetta with an even bigger grin. She went off and soon returned with Sheila's drink. "We'll catch up on the news later" she said, "when I'm not so busy! Sheila smiled and sat back savouring her drink, but we didn't remain there for very long as both of us were feeling tired after our long day. As soon as we got back to the stateroom, I nipped outside and performed in my litter igloo, washed my paws and face and retired into my comfy bed. Sheila took off her evening outfit and busied herself tidying the stateroom and seeing to the litter igloo. "That's it" she remarked, sitting on the sofa and pressing the little gadget that starts up the moving picture box, "I'm just going to catch the news and then it's bed for me too". A few minutes later and I had all but nodded off …but I was rudely awakened by that horrendous gushing water sound and saw Sheila coming out of the non bathroom. That noise was the the one thing I'd not liked about the ship so far! She went to her bed and smiled as she picked up the chocolate Pedro had left, but wasn't smiling when she turned to me with the ragged turtle in her hand. I got a sharp telling off - which I don't get from her very often I might say – so I supposed I'd have to forego any future thoughts of claw exercise in the stateroom. Not to worry, I was sure I'd find some other suitable place. My eyes wouldn't stay open any more … I slept.

First day at sea:

I was awakened by bright sunlight streaming in through the glass door as Sheila opened the curtains. I heard the rattle of my breakfast crunchy biscuits as she tipped them into my bowl, so after a quick all over stretch and the breakfast soon demolished, outside I went. I could see the sparkling blue water all around us and overhead there were one or two of those large white birds whirling about. I wondered if they'd hitched a ride from Southampton! Morning ablutions over, I strolled inside and saw Sheila had dressed and was ready to go. "Just going to have my breakfast Misty" she said, "I'll pick you up later." Off she went so I returned to the balcony and sat down to enjoy a bit of sunshine. Some time later there was a knock at the door and Pedro came in grinning at me. "'Ere you are Mistee, I 'av something nice for you" and he dropped a couple of large shrimps in my bowl. I gobbled them up - yummy! I gave him a thank you rub around the ankles and switched on my loudest purr. Swiftly he busied himself around the stateroom and in no time the big bed was made, the non bathroom cleaned, and everywhere looked spotless. Mind you, I have to say that Sheila hadn't left anything out of place. Our house in Cornwall is always very orderly and that's the reason I employ her as my housekeeper! I returned to the balcony once again and just had time for a quick cat nap before she returned. She selected another collar for me, clipped on the lead and said we were going to explore the decks outside. That sounded exciting, so I eagerly followed behind her as once more we made our way to the elevators.

This time we went upwards with the mystery lady telling us we had arrived at deck fourteen. Leaving the elevator we went outside and I could see rows and rows of chairs with people also enjoying the sunshine. Many seemed to be dressed in rather odd clothes, often brightly coloured and very brief, and in no way flattering to some of the overweight people we passed! I pride myself on being immaculate at all times and my pale grey and white catsuit fits precisely. Sheila also dresses with care and makes sure that nobody (except me!) ever sees her rather fat thighs. I know that in no way would she show off her bare legs to other people so I had no fears that she would embarrass me by dressing like some of the outrageous sights I noticed! As we passed, yes the usual cat comments, and I felt rather like royalty as I accepted many pats on the head. Soon we came to the far end of the deck and I could see a long building with big windows that reached right to the ground. Looking through them, I could see many people who seemed to be running on small roads but not getting anywhere, with others riding bicycles which also didn't appear to be moving! What a waste of time! We cats would never just stop in one place moving our paws up and down on the spot. I shook my head, you humans do have some weird habits! As we walked by, I could also see some young men with bare chests sitting down and raising their arms up and down, holding things in their paws which appeared heavy. I shook my head - each to his own I guess - but I noticed Sheila looked through the windows at the young men for a few moments. I wonder why?

Carrying on we suddenly came upon something that looked like a large rock, well more of a mountain really! Sheila looked down at me, "I think you will like this, Misty, it's the rock climbing wall." I peered upwards and could see that the wall was filled with little holes and ledges and there were four people wearing bright yellow (that unflattering colour!) round hard hats, and they seemed to be attached to long bits of string whilst very slowly trying to make their way to the top of the wall, using these holes and ledges. I could see a flag at the top waving in the wind. One of those white birds was perched by the flag. Well, the people attempting to climb were certainly taking their time about it, I thought, any competent cat could be up there and down again in a few moments! This lot looked pitiful! Sheila was chatting to a young member of the ship's crew who was standing at the foot of the wall encouraging the people clinging to its side. He patted me and said that he remembered when Sheila had brought Truffles here before and that she (Truffles, obviously, not Sheila – she couldn't climb a stepladder!) had climbed up the wall in no time. They were laughing at the memory. He turned to me "Want to have a go Misty?" he said. Why not, I thought, but I'm not having any string tied round me. I can nip up there in no time and catch that bird napping! With this in mind, I jerked the lead out of Sheila's hand and sprang up at the wall. It was so easy jumping from ledge to ledge, I didn't know why the people on it were creeping along so slowly. I sped by one man, brushing his shoulder with my tail, and noticed his eyes nearly popped out of his head! "Help!" he cried to his companions, "I'm hallucinating, I've just seen a cat go by!" He lost his footing and desperately clung to his piece of string. This stopped the other three right in their tracks, and I had a moment of guilt until I saw them unsuccessfully trying not to laugh at their friend dangling in mid air, but he soon righted himself and I heard him shout out one of those naughty words! A few moments later I reached the top but sadly the commotion below had frightened the bird away. Pity, I would have liked to have seen one close to ... maybe I'd get another chance later. It seemed very windy at the top of the wall so as I loathe getting my fur blown about, I nipped back down passing my fellow climbers who only seemed to have moved a few more centimetres on their laborious journey to the top. It'll be dark before they get there at this rate I thought scornfully. Back on the ground once again, Sheila and the crew member both smiled and he gave me a nice pat. "I think this deserves a lick of ice cream, don't you, Misty?" said Sheila and so we walked on to where there was a stand with an ice ream machine. She pressed a button and out came some of that so delicious creamy stuff which she caught in two cups, one large for her and one small for me. We strolled over to an empty chair, Sheila sitting on it, me underneath. The sun was lovely and so was the ice cream. I soon dozed off and she was chatting to the people sitting beside her. A bit later on we got up and continued our promenade.

We next passed by a water pool where several people were splashing about and obviously enjoying themselves. It was amusing to watch and by the side of the pool were some little coloured jets of water that were leaping about and making patterns. I patted them with my paw for a moment or two - pretty gingerly because I didn't want to get wet - but I couldn't catch one. I cannot for the life of me think of a more ghastly pastime than swimming! Stupid dogs like swimming, smart cats most certainly do NOT, except for our foreign cousins, the Turkish Van cats. Throw a ball or a stick into water for a dog and it will run straight in and fetch it, get itself soaking wet (ugh!) and then shake it's wet fur all over its owner! What pleasure is there in that? The dog then has to be dried off and the owner is probably not best pleased in having his own clothes sprayed with water drops! I guess Sheila must agree with me because I know that she doesn't swim. I once heard her tell someone that she swam like a stone, though I can't really say I've ever seen a stone swim even in the pond near us at home. And as I mentioned above, if she paraded round a water pool on or a crowded beach wearing a swim suit, inflicting her legs on the unsuspecting public, the place would clear immediately!

Carrying on round the upper decks, we approached what looked like a small enclosed grassy area with holes in it, each one with a little flag by it. People were walking around this course with long sticks potting little white balls into the holes. Well, this looked a lot better than swimming to me. I looked up at Sheila expectantly. She got the message and we walked up closer. It was good fun to watch and I knew right away that I could easily get the white balls into the holes without the need of a stick. I am well used to patting things about and have a good aim. I hoped we would be able to join in ourselves! My prayer was answered because suddenly two people, who were playing the game with a teenage boy, looked up and Sheila gave a gasp of surprise and greeted them saying "Well, I don't believe it, Ken, Val I never realised you were coming on this cruise! You told me you were going to Dorset!" The other two burst out laughing and said that they had decided to surprise Sheila by turning up ... but they hadn't expected to see her until in the evening! They all chatted excitedly for a few minutes and then "This is our grandson, Dylan," said Val, "as you know, Sheila, he is a junior champion golfer and so we thought we'd come up here and let him humiliate us on the putting green! Do you want to join us for a bit?" "Why not" replied Sheila, "and I think Misty here would like to pat a few balls about too!" They all laughed. I don't know why, I knew I could run rings round all three of them when it came to putting things in holes, though I wasn't too sure about young champion Dylan's capabilities! The four of them, all armed with sticks, then walked forward to the start of the course of nine holes. Sheila unclipped my lead and warned me not to run off. As if I would! Well, no I wouldn't actually, not in unknown territory like this enormous ship, and particularly as it was surrounded by water! In turn they aimed their balls at the first of the holes. Dylan started and his went right in. Val and Sheila followed, Val taking three shots and Sheila five (talk about letting the Cornish team down!) and Ken took a respectable two shots. Then they all turned and looked down at me, smiling to each other. That rather annoyed me - I'll give them something to smile about, I thought, and right from where we were standing I casually knocked the ball, using my right front paw, straight into the hole! If I had been a human I would have turned around and bowed! There was a shocked silence for a moment and then they all erupted into peals of that horrific noise you humans refer to as 'laughter' though to me it sounded more like a pack of our hyena cousins laughing! "Goodness Misty" exclaimed Sheila, "I never thought you had it in you!" Come on, I thought, let's get on with it then, you ain't seen nothing yet! So we all continued and at each of the next eight holes Dylan and I took one shot, the others anything from two to five. I don't have to tell you who was the worst! I was really enjoying myself by now, and sometimes I used my left front paw and sometimes I half turned and used one or other of my back paws, causing both admiring glances and laughs from the other people who were standing around watching. "My goodness," said one man, "does your cat perform in a circus?" More bursts of laughter! After the last hole, they gave their sticks back to a crew member who had been watching with his eyes on stalks, and sat down on some nearby seats. I curled up under Sheila's as I was quite tired by this time after my little exhibition, but I was glad I had kept my end up and shown how some cats, like me for example (!) are as good at ball games as dogs are! I do have to reluctantly admit that dogs do usually get one over cats when it comes to chasing and fetching balls, but could they get a hole in one ... I doubt it! Anyway, it was nice dozing under the chair as Sheila, Val and Ken caught up with all their news. Dylan patted me and whispered in my ear that there was already a world famous tiger who played golf, so who knows, there might be a cat golfer one day! He giggled to himself and then had gone off to play games with some other young people in something he referred to as a video games arcade ..... what that meant, I have totally no idea! But I didn't care, I was just having a great time on this lovely ship and now I was relaxing contentedly in the sun (every cat's favourite pastime) so very shortly I nodded off. It has always been my aim to sleep 22 hours out of 24, but ever since I've been on the ship with all the new mind blowing new experiences, I havn't come anywhere near my goal since we left home!

I was rudely awakened by Sheila from a dream where I was just on the point of catching one of those white sea birds, so I wasn't in the best of humours as we set off towards the other end of the deck. Val and Ken must have left whilst I was asleep. Pity, I rather liked them. "Now Misty" said Sheila, "we are coming to something called the FlowRider, but I'm not sure that you will find it your cup of tea!" She laughed. What IS she on about now, I wondered, cups of tea – she knows I don't drink tea! And what's a flow rider? Well, I was about to find out! As we approached, I saw several people watching what looked like an enclosed small raging, foaming river where two or three people were taking it in turns attempting to stand on little boards on top of these seething, boiling waves of water! Ah, I thought, perhaps that's what she meant by cup of tea … maybe the foaming water was used to make tea. How stupid, a kettle is much easier. We edged a bit closer, me keeping carefully out of the way of the spray blowing towards us. "Wow" said Sheila, "I wouldn't dare do that!" No dear, as you can't swim, you'd have no chance, and it's certainly something no sane cat would want to do … still, as I said earlier, each to his own! The people using the FlowRider were obviously having the time of their lives, whooping and shouting and the crowd were cheering if they successfully reached the end of the run, or ooohing if they fell into the raging torrent. I must say it was exciting to watch, rather like watching the final of our local cat tree climbing contest when some of the more daring toms in the area risk life and limb clinging to the thinnest twigs right at the top of the trees. I've seen a few nasty falls during that contest, but luckily here nobody who fell into the water hurt anything except their pride.

A little later we left and, back at the elevators again, we caught one down to deck ten and home. I had a refreshing drink of water and went outside to sit in my sunny corner of the balcony, and Sheila went off to have her lunch somewhere. Having assured myself that no large white bird was lurking in the corner waiting to be captured (well, it seems that dreams rarely do come true!) I lay down, had a nice relaxing ear scratch, then an all over stretch and turned on my sleep mode control … maybe I'd get on the way to my 22 hours sleep!

Waking up a while later, I went to look through the glass wall out to sea. I have to say it again, but I was blown away by the sight of all this blue water surrounding us. It was something I just never could have imagined in my life. It struck me that there must be a whole new, enormous world outside of our garden in Cornwall and how lucky I was that this cruise company had allowed me to see some of it. As I was sitting daydreaming, I heard the stateroom door open and Sheila came back. She looked pleased with herself and I saw she was carrying a bag from which she produced a teddy bear wearing a nautical vest with the name of the ship on it. Oh dear, I thought, as she kissed him on the nose and sat him on the wall unit, how soppy can you get! "A new friend for you Misty" she smiled, "I'm going to call him Captain." She disappeared into the non bathroom and I looked gloomily at Captain – he was only the first one she'd succumbed to; I felt he would soon have his own little crew of bears joining him during this trip!

Sheila sat down and switched on the picture machine on the wall, staying there watching it for a while as she flicked me over some crunchy treats. Then she got up and fetched my lead. "Come on Misty" she said, "Now I'm going to show you around the upper outside deck. I will be ashore tomorrow and you will have to stay in the stateroom so we will go out now." Yet more new sights to cram into my day, I thought, whatever next! Down our usual path to the elevators and this time we went up to deck fifteen, according to the unseen lady. As we stepped outside the sun was blinding and really quite hot already. I could see rows and rows of people lounging on their low seats enjoying the sunshine. Everybody we passed seemed in a good mood and several made the usual cat comments and patted me. I have to say I was loving all the attention! A bit of sun cheers everybody up, both human and animal, and makes all the difference doesn't it? In Cornwall lately it's been nothing but rain, rain and more rain and the skies have been generally pale grey with just a bit of white showing - exactly the colour of my fur come to think of it!

We walked past another large water pool, this one had a glass roof over it and even more comfy seats and sofas placed around the edges. There were some pretty coloured water spouts dancing up and down at one end as we passed by, which fascinated me. Sheila thoughtfully stopped and had a chat with some people sitting nearby whilst I attempted to catch one of the water spouts but with no success I'm afraid … Carrying on and up some steps we then came across something that totally bowled me over … GRASS! I blinked, what the … ? But yes it really was REAL grass … GROWING grass! Unbelievable! Sheila smiled and said that she had kept the best till last! We approached said grass and I sank my paws into it, lovely. Oh yes … I lay down and had a lovely roll over. Everyone around laughed! I could see that people were in groups, some playing on the grass with balls, others sitting in wicker chairs by the side of it drinking those naughty cocks' tails and even a few sitting on the grass with baskets containing bottles of that red and white stuff you also like to drink, plus cheeses and other interesting looking titbits. I love cheese. Maybe if I encouraged Sheila to walk over towards them, I could grab a piece. I was in luck as suddenly a couple recognised Sheila and called us over. "Oh, hi Petra and Graham" said Sheila, "Great to see you again … how are you keeping?" She sat down and I immediately sidled up to Petra - she looked as if she liked cats! I was right because Sheila introduced me and told me Petra and Graham had known Truffles and had read her books! Good, I thought, I will be able to have a nice rest here on the grass whilst they are all talking. I looked up at Petra and then pointedly at her piece of cheese and, yes, it worked because she gave me some bits which I eagerly devoured and then, with her stroking my back … oh so soothing to a cat … I soon dozed off on the comfortable grass.

Some time later Sheila, or maybe Petra, shook me awake and

they said their "goodbyes" and "see you laters", and we strolled on again. Suddenly there was a shout and I looked up and saw Sheila's friend Michael – or Mr Pumpkin as I like to call him – waving to us from the opposite side of the grass. There was so much grass that to me it looked like a park! He was with quite a large group of people and he seemed to be teaching them some kind of game where they were throwing soft bean bags at two boards each with a hole in it. Rather like the cats' game of toss a snail into a bird's nest. We crossed the grass and Sheila asked him what the game was called as she had never seen it before. "Baggo" he replied, "Come and have a go!" "No" she smiled, "we'll just watch for a bit. I don't want to make a fool of myself!" She sat down on one of the wicker chairs, and released my lead so I could I curl up on the lovely grass. Mmmm, it felt good! Suddenly Sheila sat up and once more I heard her saying that she couldn't believe it, how are you etc. Must be somebody else she knows I thought and looked up to see a very nice looking young man with the biggest smile I'd seen yet approaching us. They exchanged hugs and then he leant down and said "Hi Misty, you're pretty, I've heard all about you!" (Oh it's so nice to be popular isn't it?!) Sheila told me afterwards that his name was Dev and he ran one of the cocks' tails bars on board and that she'd known him now for several years. Well they were certainly talking like old friends, but he was working so couldn't stop for too long. "Campari?" he said laughing. "Naturally!" she replied, so when he passed by a few minutes later he brought her a glass. Revolting smelling stuff I've always thought, but she likes it and, indeed, told me once that as she sails so often on this ship, whenever she arrives at a bar where somebody she knows is serving, a Campari is always miraculously awaiting her! Well, with me, whenever I approach my dinner bowl at home, there's always my favourite food ready for me in it too. Just proof of the excellent service and attention I get at home, and that she gets on the ship! That's the life, eh!

Sheila had her eyes half closed in the bright sun, so I took the opportunity to move further out on to the grass where I could see some people playing some sort of game where they were rolling large black balls towards a little white ball. That looks fun I thought, and crept a bit nearer. A couple of people, also lounging in nearby wicker chairs, spoke to me and got out their little speaking/picture making machines and took some photos. I was beginning to feel like a real celebrity now, like Truffles, so I preened myself and let them pat me, favouring them with one of my best purrs! But the little white ball was proving very tempting, so I quickly nipped across to where it was now surrounded by six of the black balls and with a quick flick of my paw, knocked it away ...much to the surprise of the people playing the game who didn't look as happy (I don't know why!) as the people watching! But a few seconds later as the spectators dissolved into hoots of your hyena like laughter, even the players joined suit. Everyone seemed in hysterics! Well, I didn't care ... this was fun! I patted the little white ball to and fro several times across the grass but finally reluctantly returned, plus ball, back to Sheila who had now roused herself and was calling for me in not too happy a tone! Come on dear, it's only a game ... don't be a spoilsport! "Misty" she said, "You've thoroughly embarrassed me! Naughty girl ... give me the ball!" OK, OK keep your fur on, I mumbled to myself, and rolled the ball to her feet. She returned it to the people on the grass .. "I'm so sorry" she said, "your game has been ruined." "Don't worry" one of the players replied, "It's been a sight for sore eyes, we certainly didn't expect to find a cat on board nicking our ball!" And once more they all fell about laughing. Anyway, nobody seemed too upset, so I don't know why Sheila was getting so worked up about it all – take a chill pill dear! Anyway, after she had apologised yet again, she picked me up and returned to her seat. My lead was firmly attached and I sat by her feet once more, feeling a sulk coming on. She had spoiled my fun. Why? Nobody else had seemed to mind. The people next door introduced themselves as June and Roger and said they had enjoyed the whole episode and then, whilst I continued with my sulk, they all started chatting away and I heard them arrange to meet up with Sheila later before dinner in the Martini Bar. What's a Martini Bar I wondered vaguely, but then sleep overcame me once more!

I was awakened by Sheila gently tugging at my collar. "Come on" she said, "we're going back now. We'll pass the Hot Glass Show on the way, Misty, but I've seen it before – it's fascinating but nothing you would understand! Anyway," she went on, "I can't stop as it's nearly time for my afternoon canapés!" I wondered what a hot glass show was and what on earth canapés were, hopefully perhaps something to eat? We strolled back along the deck again, though I was sorry to leave the grass. At the hot glass show there were some passengers sitting on rows of benches all intently watching two or three people who were blowing down long tubes – what a strange thing to do I thought! On the end of each tube was a coloured blob of something that looked sticky, and as I watched the blobs seemed to continually change shape! Curious. Well, they say curiosity killed the cat don't they, but in this case as the people who were holding these shimmering blobs kept dipping them into a rather hot and frightening fire, it was all slightly unnerving, so I didn't mind that Sheila didn't stop!

Back in the stateroom, Sheila had only just sat down and poured herself a glass of bubbly when there was a knock at the door and there was another smiley faced young man who gave Sheila a covered plate. She placed it on the low table and I could immediately smell something fishy! Mmmm ... if these were the mysterious canapés, they sounded just up my alley! (and readers, no I've never been an alley cat myself!) I stood up on my hind legs and patted at the edge of the table, looking expectantly up at her with my best wistful expression. This always works! "Yes, yes" she smiled, "I suppose I havn't got any chance of having the prawns all to myself have I?" No dear, you havn't! Lid removed, there were four huge prawns plus some other interesting looking things. Well, I got two of the prawns in the end and something else which also tasted nice but I didn't know what it was! So, contented once more, I washed my whiskers and retired for another catnap. Sheila switched on the picture machine...

Some time later I awoke to the sound of flushing water coming from the non bathroom and a while after Sheila appeared dressed in another evening outfit. "I'm going to order your dinner now Misty" she said reaching for the speaking gadget by the bed. I was still coming around from my cosy sleep but heard clearly enough the magic words salmon and chicken. Mmmm, can't be bad I thought. I felt a purr of anticipation coming on. After reaching into the very small cupboard above the larger cupboard and retrieving some sparkling bits and pieces which she placed on her wrists and fingers, Sheila sat down on the sofa and I perched beside her on my cushion. We sat there for a few minutes, she idly stroking me and me counting down the seconds until my dinner arrived! When it did, brought in by yet another smiley faced young man, it was definitely worth waiting for folks! First some quite mouth watering rolls of smoked salmon garnished with yummy prawns and then chicken pieces in tasty gravy sauce. I don't think I have ever cleared my bowls so fast before! Sheila laughed, "If that's what they will be serving you this trip, Misty, you will go home a proper little porker!" And you, dear, will go home the size of a baby elephant I thought! After a comforting burp - yes I guess I DID eat it too fast - following all that lovely food, a quick visit to the litter igloo was in order before I settled down in my bed for a nice after dinner sleep. Sheila sighed and quickly tidied up after me, grumbling that why did I have to go just as she was ready to leave and not earlier – but these things can't be planned just for HER convenience, can they? "I'm off now Misty" she called over her shoulder as she went to the door, "I'm meeting June and Roger for a drink in the Martini Bar and then going for my own dinner. Be good while I'm gone!" As if I wouldn't be!!

I was intending to have a nice sleep but somehow I couldn't nod off - too many new experiences had happened to me today, things I never could have imagined, and I just couldn't get my head round them.

Suddenly I heard someone come in and it was Pedro. "Ello Mistee" he smiled and patted me, "Ere you are, I have a nice squeed for you tonight!" A rather delicious smelling fishy item dropped by my side. I had never heard of a 'squeed' before but it certainly tasted good! I switched on my purr at its loudest volume and idly watched as Pedro carried out his excellent duties turning down Sheila's bed and placing her chocolate on the pillow, and this time he made what looked like one of those big white birds out of the fluffy rag, sorry towel, he took from the non bathroom. I made a mental note to have a gentle scratch on it later (on its underside) so that Sheila wouldn't notice!

When he had finished, he came and sat down beside me and said "You must be very good girl Mistee because my boss he comes here soon to inspect things. It is all to do with 'elf and safety and specially because YOU are here." Well, of course I know I am pretty special but I wondered what exactly I had to do with an elf? I think they are something like our Cornish piskies at home. Also I had never met another boss before ... it's ME who is the boss in our house! Anyway, I was soon to find out who Pedro's boss was because only a few minutes later another important looking man entered, wearing a smart dark blue jacket with gold stripes on the sleeves.

Pedro jumped up and told his boss that everything was all in order. The boss smiled and bent down towards me. "Hello" he said, "You're pretty, what's your name? My name is Tom and I am the Hotel Director on this ship." "This is Mistee" said Pedro. Tom patted me and if I could have spoken human I would have told him that I am the House Director of Sheila's home in Cornwall! So I gave him a brief purr and then retreated to my bed. Tom and Pedro went all round the stateroom and balcony and Tom noted that my litter igloo, with sack of litter and pack of disposal bags beside it, was neatly placed in the corner of the balcony and because, as I think I've mentioned before, both Sheila and I are extremely fussy, everything was totally – as Pedro said – in order. Sheila said once that hygiene was a very important feature of this ship, and one of the reasons she keeps cruising on it is because how spotless and gleaming everything is. At any rate, Tom seemed very pleased with his inspection and a relieved Pedro smiled like a Cheshire cat as he was given top marks. "Well, I've never seen a cat on here before, it's a first for me! So long Misty" smiled Tom as he left the stateroom. What a funny expression I thought, I don't think I am particularly 'long'. Yet another of your strange human sayings I suppose! "Adios Mistee" said Pedro and he also left the stateroom. After my promised scratch on the towelling bird, I sank back in bed and this time sleep did overcome me!

I awoke later as Sheila returned. She was smiling. "Well Misty, I've had a good time this evening … a drink with June and Roger in the Martini Bar, and then after dinner I went to the Champagne Bar with a nice guy on my table called Richard. He is extremely knowledgeable – sorry Misty, to you that means he is clever – about ships and simply everything to do with cruising and so we had a very interesting conversation." (Ah, "knowledgeable" another new word to add to my store of your human words!) "I don't want the evening to end yet," she

68

continued, " so I think we'll go to the casino!" What on earth is a 'casino' I wondered. I watched as she opened the little cupboard again and took out three twenty dollar money notes, and then she picked out one of my glittery evening collars, slipped it on me, clipped on the wretched lead and off we went. Casino, here we come!

After the usual stroll to the elevator, we fell downwards - this time to Deck Four according to the unseen lady. Would I ever see her in the flesh? Walking past the shops we entered a large area full of people, with lots of musical noises and human chatter going on. It was quite loud and somewhat scary to a little cat like me, though I wasn't going to show it, so I kept close to Sheila's ankles. A good many of them were sitting round tables playing with cards or little round discs, but even more were sitting in front of noisy machines which rattled and bleeped continuously and at odd times made even louder bleeps which seemed to make the person playing with them shout or wave their arms about excitedly. Just what was all this? It was like a reunion of the Cornish Cats United Club at Christmas!

After weaving up and down several lines of these machines, Sheila at last stopped at one. "Ah, this was lucky for me last time" she muttered. The man playing on the machine next door gave a double take on seeing me, but I was used to that now! "I heard there was someone with a cat on board" he said, " well, let's hope she brings us some luck!" They both laughed and Sheila pulled out a tall seat and sat down hooking my lead to its leg. "Come on now, Misty, yes, bring me luck!" she chuckled, let's give it a go, though I expect it'll need feeding up for a couple of days before it'll pay out much!" I idly wondered what she was going to feed the machine with, I hadn't noticed her bringing any bits of salmon with her! Then I saw her put two of the twenty dollar money notes into it! Aaah, so these machines eat your money do they? Now I come to think of it, I vaguely remember that last time she returned from the ship she said something about how she had been very lucky in the casino and come out with enough money to pay off her ship's bill, but that the time before the machines had just eaten all her money right up! Seems a bit risky to me chancing your money; still at least if she loses it she won't be able to get too many more teddy bears! I can never get my head around you humans and money ... you always seem to be wanting it, and then when you get it you give it away to all those tempting shops and, now I realised, also to these strange places called casinos!

I looked around me, but all I could see were people's backs – and bums – sitting on the seats facing the line of machines behind us. Everyone was in a good mood, you could feel it ... this was obviously a happy place on the ship, despite the fact that you might lose all your money! I settled down to watch to see how Sheila got on! She started pressing a button on the front of the machine, and then kept repeating it. Each time she pressed the button, little pictures that were dotted all over the machine's face spun round and round. That looked fun! I pawed at Sheila's knee. "Oh come on then, you can sit on my knee if you want" she said and hoisted me up. I watched intently, sometimes three pictures that looked the same would arrive in a line together and the machine played happy music and at other times no pictures matched and I would hear Sheila sighing. Suddenly the machine made a louder sound and all the pictures started madly to roll around. A voice said what sounded like "fifteen free spins" and different music started to play. Sheila sat back and the little pictures then went totally mad spinning non stop. I pawed the machine's face but I couldn't catch one! The man sitting beside Sheila laughed. "Come on puss, bring your mum some luck!" "I wish!" replied Sheila. At the end of the fifteen spins, from Sheila's expression I gathered that she hadn't exactly made her fortune, but then she said she'd made a bit of profit so that was it, enough for now, she'd cash it in and keep it for the next evening. "Very sensible" nodded her neighbour, as she pressed another button and a slip of paper emerged. "Come on Misty, time for a nightcap coffee" said Sheila and that was my introduction to the casino.

During the cruise we went in there most nights – Sheila seemed to win a bit and lose a bit but I can report that at the end of the cruise she did go home a winner with an extra ten of those twenty dollar money notes over what she started with, so she was well pleased! We then took ourselves to the frothy coffee lounge, where Violetta served Sheila with her favourite café latte and Amoretto bedtime drink. Yuk! Then back to our comfortable stateroom again. What was to come next I mewsed as I sat on the litter igloo. After checking that Sheila had cleaned and refreshed it, I sank into bed and watched as she sank into hers … fortunately she didn't remark on the bird … and so we both slept!

The next day:

The next morning the sun had put his hat on for us ... it was bright and lovely. I could feel that we were not moving so when Sheila was messing about in the non bathroom, I wandered outside onto the balcony and looked through the glass wall. Yes, we had stopped and far below I could see people, looking the size of ants from right up here, scurrying about beside the ship. Several long motor machines were waiting and I could see lines of people getting into them. I wondered where they were off to. I could see other ships too, some with people getting off them like ours, and some that seemed to be piled high with big boxes, and those tall metal monsters with chains and hooks - like I had seen at Southampton - seemed very busy! I could also see across the water a big statue that looked like a lady human with a fish's tail! Strange! I was peering at this when along came a group of the big white sea birds and sat on her head! I wished one of them would sit on mine ...

Sheila called me from inside saying that my breakfast was ready. No views of birds or fishy ladies would stop me from my breakfast, so I nipped back in pretty sharpish. It was my own food Sheila had brought for my breakfasts, not the posh dinners I now decided that I could quite well become accustomed to on the ship (!) but give it to her, at least it wasn't "own brand", she had got the decent stuff! Cod and haddock with shrimp sauce this morning! After I'd finished, it was the usual visit to the litter igloo and whisker cleaning session whilst she finished the daily palaver of fiddling with her face and hair.

"Right Misty" she said, "I'm off to breakfast now and then I'll be ashore. So you be a good girl, sit outside and enjoy the sun. I'll be back for a late lunch and then we can go out on the grass again and see what's happening up there. Then I've got a ticket to go the ice show. You like skating!" And off she went smiling to herself. Everything she said had gone right over my head ... well, she IS a lot taller than me, ha! ha! What did she mean by saying she was a shore? What's a shore? I thought she was a person! And DO I like skating? I wasn't certain what that meant either. Oh well, I guessed I'd find out eventually. I returned to the balcony and lay down in my corner in the sun. Shortly after she'd gone, Pedro appeared. Somehow he always seems to know when she has gone out so that he can come in and do his stateroom tasks without disturbing her. "Ello Mistee pusseecat" he smiled, stroking my head, "'Ow are you today?" I nudged his hand, because I could see something in it, and sure enough he had a lovely prawn for me!. I purred at full volume and rubbed his ankles which seemed to please him. I was glad – he is such a nice man. I lay dozing comfortably as he carried out his morning duties, and after he'd left I fell properly asleep.

Not for long though ... I was suddenly awakened by the sound of screeching and there perched on the outer rail over the glass wall were four or five of the white sea birds, all squabbling amongst themselves. They didn't look as if they'd noticed me in my corner. Good! I remained very still and kept my eyes peeled. Unlike the sea birds at Southampton, these ones' wings were topped with black. Maybe they were nautical style magpies? You never know! Still they hadn't noticed me as they seemed to be having an almighty argument between themselves. I wondered if I could take this chance of a lifetime and nab one. Well, it certainly wouldn't do any harm to try ... so keeping flat to the deck I slowly slunk forward. Still they continued with their rowdy screeching and now they were also pecking at each other. Now was my moment, so I launched myself up at the group hissing, growling and brandishing my claws, looking as fierce as I can (which is difficult because at heart I am a peaceable ladylike cat, not a fighting tom!) But, oh dear, I had misjudged the height of the glass wall and to my great humiliation I crashed into the top and slithered back down to fall in an untidy heap at the bottom. The birds all screeched in unison and in great confusion flapped up in the air, feathers flying everywhere, and soon were out of sight! Oh well, if nothing else I had ended their argument for them! But, dear readers, am I ever going to be able to catch a bird? I fear not. I had just missed out on the best opportunity ever! Well, I wasn't going to let it upset my wonderful cruise so I would just have try to forget the incident. But as I stamped back across to my cushion, I was definitely not in the best of moods I can tell you! Well, sleep cures everything so that's what I did next!

Eventually Sheila returned to the stateroom carrying a large bag which she dropped down on the sofa before disappearing into the non bathroom from where I heard the horrendous flushing noise and the sound of her washing her paws. "Ah, that's better!" she said and sat down on the sofa, leaning down and patting me. "Well, I've had a lovely morning Misty, I hope you've had a nice time too." (I smiled grimly to myself) "I'll just about be in time for lunch so I'll quickly give you yours and then I'll be off." I brightened up at the anticipation of lunch! "I've always loved Copenhagen" she continued, "but it is VERY expensive, so I had to rein in my spending a bit!" But I bet you still bought a teddy bear I thought. And, yes I was right, because she then brought two, thankfully small, teddies out of the bag! One had a red tee shirt on with a white heart saying Copenhagen on it, the other a white tee shirt with Denmark on it. All I could think was thank God she doesn't make me wear a tee shirt with Misty or Cornwall on the front of it! She emptied the bag of a few other items, and then after putting the bears on the shelf with the others, gave me my lunchtime crunchy treats and went off for her lunch.

After demolishing the treats, I returned to the balcony, now in a much better frame of mind. There were no birds in sight except for one large all black bird sitting on top of the fishy lady's head. But I put all thoughts of birds out of my mind and instead wondered what we would be doing next on the ship. It did sound as if Sheila was going to take me out onto that nice patch of grass. That would be nice. I lay down and dozed …

Sheila returned full of smiles. She'd obviously enjoyed her lunch too! She joined me on the balcony, sat down on the long chair and I perched on her knee purring. I got the feeling that if she were a cat, she'd be purring too. I can read her like a book, and as usual I was right! "Well Misty" she said, "at lunch I met up with two friends of mine, Mary and Eric, who I met on here last year. I didn't know they were on this cruise so that was a nice surprise. I expect you'll meet them sometime later. Their daughter has a lovely dog - a poodle - who is called Misty as well!" She chuckled.

A dog? A dog? Called Misty? MY name given to a lowly DOG! I couldn't believe it … and I thought I was the ONLY Misty! My tail twitched irritably. I think Sheila must have read my mind too for she cuddled me and said "Never mind Misty, don't get prickly now, you are the only one for me!" After a few minutes of being petted and cuddled, my hurt feelings had recovered and when she said we would go on deck now, I jumped down and eagerly ran inside. She put on my nautical collar, clipped on the lead and we made our way to the elevator bank.

As we stepped out on to the big grassy space, I felt much better … the sky was blue, the sun was smiling at us from on high and the grass looked lovely! I tugged at the lead but Sheila held on tightly. She sat down on one of the wicker chairs near to the bar, looping the lead round its leg, so I lay down just in front of her and had a luxurious rollover on the grass. Up came the young man with the truly big smile - everyone who worked on this ship seemed to be permanently smiling, but he had the biggest smile ever! "Hi Dev" said Sheila, "Do you know, I really fancy one of your Pussyfoot cocktails, you make them so delicious!" "Coming right up" he replied, giving me a pat, "and here's a pussy with four feet!" He strolled away laughing. I wondered what a Pussyfoot was, surely not puréed cats paws! Ugh! No way, anyway Sheila wouldn't eat or drink anything made of her favourite animal, the cat! I lay back but kept one eye open to see what Dev would bring. He was back in a few minutes carrying a tall glass with a pale orangey coloured liquid in it that looked reddish at the bottom, and with a straw and a sprig of leaves and cherries stuck on the top. Sheila immediately had a long pull on the straw. "Mmmm, lovely!" she said. They chatted for a few minutes before he went off again making drinks for the other people sitting around us. Really this was a very nice happy and relaxed place and everyone was enjoying themselves. Sheila idly chatted to the couple sitting alongside her, and the lady knelt down and gave me a lovely tummy rub! Bliss! I felt I could stay on this ship for ever ... sorry Cornwall, no disrespect!

Some while later, up we got and wandered over to the other side of the grass where I could see another group of people playing some sort of game that was being supervised by my shiny headed pal, Michael aka Mr Pumpkin! "Hi Sheila" he said, "Hi Misty". "What on earth is this game called?" asked Sheila, "I've never seen it before." "It's called Blongo" he replied. We stood and watched as one of the players picked up two of those little white golf balls that I had played with earlier, but these two were tied together with a piece of rope. In front of him was a frame with three poles and it seemed that the players had to throw the joined together balls at the frame and depending on which pole it wrapped itself around, you scored points accordingly! The man threw the balls at the frame and somehow the rope, and the balls, twisted around the centre pole. "Two points" said Michael, "Good play!"

I thought this looked quite a good game, so the next time somebody aimed at the frame, I prepared myself to leap at it and try to catch the balls. Big mistake! As Sheila was watching and talking to Michael at the same time, so didn't have her eye on me, I took my chance and tried to jerk the lead out of her hand. All this achieved was that I nearly strangled myself and the howl I gave put the player off his aim so the roped balls flew up in the air and crashed down onto a nearby table demolishing the drinks and glasses that were on it. Whoops! The lady sitting at the table then got very angry as some of the drink had splashed on to her leg - and the fact that everyone around was laughing, except for the man who threw the balls, didn't help! While Michael calmed the lady down, Sheila dragged me over to apologise to both her and the man playing the game, and I humbly held my head and put on my best pathetic expression. Fortunately this worked and the lady then smiled and patted me and all she said was that accidents would happen and this would be something she could tell her friends about back home ... a cat causing chaos on a ship! The man gave a wry grin, "Well," he said, "I was losing anyway so now the game is a draw so the cat helped me in a way!" Laughs from the other people! Michael called Dev and he quickly cleared up the broken glasses and replaced the drinks, the game continued and everyone was happy! Apart from Sheila who sighed and said "That was naughty, Misty, you really mustn't spoil other people's games!" Well, I thought, maybe next time YOU could play a game with me on the grass, then I wouldn't NEED to gatecrash other games! Strangely enough, as if she'd read my thoughts, she then said "We'll have a game of fetch the ball when there's not so many people around, now come on, it's time to go to the ice show!" So, off we went!

After another ride downwards in the elevator, the unseen lady told us we were at Deck Two and out we got to find a line of people that seemed to stretch both ahead and behind the elevator for ever! Well, this skating thing must be popular I thought! We joined the line but soon two big doors opened at the front of the line and we all moved forward quite quickly after that. Passing through the doors, suddenly I felt a chill in the air and was glad of my fur coat. Sheila found a seat about three rows from the front and sat down with me on her knee, and judging by the way some of the people sitting in front of us were pulling on sweaters, they felt chilly too! This place looked rather like the theatre to me except that in the centre was a large square that was white. The rows of seats were around three sides of this square. We waited a little while while the place filled up, Sheila having the usual conversation with the people each side of her about me, so I collected a few more pats! Then the lights dimmed, music started and the audience collectively looked towards the white square.

Suddenly the square was filled with whirling figures in amazing sparkly and colourful outfits, all spinning and jumping and the mewsic (sorry, you say music!) was so lively it made everyone watching want to dance! NOW I knew what Sheila meant when she said I would like skating! On Winter Saturday nights - on the moving picture box she looks at - THAT'S where I've seen the same sort of figures! And the catchy music too - I like music and Sheila bobs me up and down in time to it when there's a particular tune she likes. She calls this Cat Dancing! Over these past months her favourite has been a tune called 'Get Lucky' so I've listened to that so many times, and bounced so much I've never needed to go on a diet! In fact I like that tune too so I hoped they'd play it now during this show! (Sadly they didn't!)

The next hour or so was a constant stream of great music and amazing actions from the colourful skaters that had the audience clapping and cheering and at the end everyone stood up and the noise was deafening! Well, what an experience! I totally loved it! I miaowed along to the music as lots of the people were doing, and I could tell that everyone was really happy and enjoying themselves! As we left the place, everyone was saying how good it was! Sheila was telling the people next door that she had never been to an ice show on land, just on this ship, and it was something she'd not forget. Well, dear readers, I wouldn't forget it either! Whatever next was going to happen on this mind boggling cruise ship experience!

We went back the same way we'd been before, but at a snail's pace as there were crowds of people milling around. So many people were waiting for the elevator that Sheila tugged on my lead and said we'd be quicker going up the stairs. Well, no effort for me - a few pants and puffs from her as we climbed up three floors - and arrived again by the glass bridge at the start of the shopping street. "Come on Misty" she said, "I'm going in to Ben and Jerry's to get an ice cream. I'll sit outside so you can have a lick too." Mmmm, yummy … I'm up for that I thought. She picked out a coffee and pistachio flavour for herself, and a plain vanilla one for me. Pity they don't make a fish flavour, but not to worry … vanilla is OK! She settled herself outside on a tall seat and put a cardboard dish underneath on the floor for me. Both of us then enjoyed a blissful few moments …

I looked up to hear Sheila talking with her friends Mary and Eric who happened to be passing by. Mary leaned down and gave me a nice pat so I switched on my purr in stereo mode. She is a nice lady and loves animals, I can tell. They all agreed to meet for drinks (yes, those sickly smelling coloured cocks' tails you all love!) in the Elite Members' lounge in an hour or so, and after they'd gone on by, Sheila got up, chucked our now empty dishes into the bin and we made our way back to the stateroom.

I returned to my favourite corner on the balcony whilst she spent the next half hour pondering on what to wear that evening, what bag and shoes to match up with it, and what appropriate sparkly bits etc. Phew, what a palaver, SO much easier to have just the one bespoke fitted fur catsuit that is suitable for all occasions just with a simple change of collar! But she seems to enjoy this fussing about what to wear and I know she prides herself that she never wears the same outfit twice on a ship – no wonder poor Tony nearly puts his back out carting her luggage about and loading it in and out of his taxi! Some people seem to manage with just a kittybag over their shoulders, Sheila can't seem to manage with less than four cases just for fourteen days! Ridiculous!

Eventually after having dozed off, I heard her approaching. I opened one eye. "Now then Misty", she said, "Your dinner should be arriving any minute and then I'm off for my meeting with Mary and Eric and after that I will be going on to my own dinner and then I'm going to see the show as there's a very good comedian on tonight. Waste of time you going, there's nothing spectacular to watch but tomorrow, now that's a different kettle of fish." What on earth has a kettle of fish got to do with things I wondered, what's she going on about now, and why would you put fish in a kettle anyway … to make fish tea? That would appeal to me but not to you lot I guess! Oh well, just another ambiguous (yes, a BIG word that I have only quite recently added to my vocabulary!) human expression that I couldn't get my head around. "Tomorrow night" she continued, "is formal night and there is going to be a truly spectacular show which you will love! My friend, Peng Fei, will be performing in it and doing some amazing acrobatics. You'll see! And I will be dining on the Captain's table as he is also a friend of mine (Oooh, get you I thought!) so if you are lucky you might be able to meet him afterwards." Blimey, it's all going to happen tomorrow I told myself, just as well I can have a quiet night in now! I idly wondered how long it would take her to get ready for this momentous sounding evening tomorrow - she'd probably start getting ready after lunch!

Sure enough, at that moment there was a knock at the door and a smiley faced young man arrived holding a tray with two little dishes on it that smelt very tasty indeed. I eagerly jumped up at him and he laughingly put them down on the balcony floor for me. "Smoked salmon nibbles followed by duck breast fillet" he said over his shoulder to Sheila as he left the room. "Your dinners are almost as good as mine, Misty" she said, "enjoy!" And believe you me, dear reader, I sure did enjoy!!!

Sheila having departed, I went back to my comfortable doze in the last of the evening sun and was lost to the world until Pedro appeared for his evening rituals. "Ello Mistee" he said,

"Another squeed for you tonight!" I gave him a grateful ankle rub, switching on the purr control, and enjoyed a few nice moments savouring the said "squeed" whilst he went around the stateroom whistling quietly to himself and leaving it in its usual pristine condition! I decided that when we got home, I would insist that Sheila steps up her own house cleaning standards to those on this ship. Although I have to admit she does keep the house very clean and always tidy, I can't say that it literally 'sparkles' like this ship seems to! After Pedro had given me a nice tummy rub and lots of pats, he left to carry on his good work in the next door stateroom, so I nipped up on the bed and surveyed the latest animal that he had made out of the fluffy white rags. I wasn't really certain exactly what it was … either a sea lion or a bulldog perhaps … but whatever, it was quite easy for me to reach underneath its tummy and have a good old claw stretch and scratch. I surveyed it afterwards, no she'd never notice it had been tampered with, particularly if she'd had several of those naughty cocks' tails!

I decided to stay indoors so curled up in my comfy bed, had a relaxing stretch and an all over licking session and then slept … it was much later that Sheila returned. She seemed to be very cheery and I think this was probably because yes she had had several of the naughty cocks' tails! "Well, that was a really enjoyable evening Misty" she said sitting down on the sofa, picking me up and putting me on her knee. "Mary, Eric and I had a nice cocktail or two before dinner (yes dear, I can see that!) and then we met up afterwards in the theatre and the guy was just so funny the whole audience fell apart laughing! (oh dear, sounds like one of Pedro's animals doesn't it … they tend to fall apart when Sheila moves them off the bed!) "After the show we ended up in the café for a nightcap" she went on, "so all in all, a really good day don't you think, Misty?" I agreed, yes it had been a great day - well each day on here seems to get better than the last one – so I wondered what tomorrow would bring! What she had mentioned earlier sounded pretty exciting to me.

We both then carried out our bedtime preparations – me to the litter igloo and her to the non bathroom. And then getting into our respective beds, we slept! What would the next day bring I mewsed – sorry, mused?

The next port of call:

The next morning dawned bright and sunny again. Performing my morning ablutions, I gazed out through the glass wall of the balcony and saw we were right next door to another big ship, not as big as ours though! Again, I saw way down below several lines of those long motor machines and people were coming off both ships and getting inside them. I wondered where they were going. We appeared to be not far from another very big town, at least as big as the previous port where I had seen the statue of the fish lady. But there was no similar statue in the water here as far as I could see. There were lots of big buildings in the distance and rows of smaller brightly coloured houses nearer to the water's edge where I thought I could see a kind of stone road crossing over the top of the water ... I suppose you would walk across it to reach them. Pity I wasn't going to be allowed off the ship to see some of these strange new places, but, on the other paw, it might also be a bit frightening when you consider I've never really been out of our back garden at home!

After Sheila had sorted out the litter igloo and given me my breakfast she went off for her own and I sat outside to do a bit of birdwatching. Several of those big white birds were flying around and some all black ones too, but none came really near our ship. Pity. Pedro duly arrived, plus two big shrimps (!) and I enjoyed having my usual morning pats from him. He bustled about in his efficient manner and within only a few minutes, all was done and dusted and he left not long before Sheila returned, but almost immediately she went out again saying she would be back just after lunchtime. Oh well, thanks for the company I thought irritably and stamped outside again. I soon wished I hadn't because all of a sudden I heard a sort of rushing water sound and some heavy drops of water fell on my head. Looking up I could see some sort of moving platform with a crew member on it who appeared to be squirting water at the stateroom windows! Before I realised just exactly how close he was, a sudden squirt totally drenched me from head to tail!

Hell's teeth ... I leapt in the air giving a loud screech and flew back inside narrowly avoiding another soaking as the platform continued on its slow route past. From the safety behind the glass doors I peeped out and saw that the whole of the floor outside was now soaking wet and full of puddles and what's more, my cushion and litter igloo were wet too! But blow them I thought furiously, look at ME ... look at my fur, ruined, sopping wet! My previous irritability escalated into a really bad temper now and as I shook and shook myself to try and get dry again, I was growling under my breath. After shaking like fury for about five minutes I gave up and decided to sit outside in the sun to try and dry my catsuit, but it was hopeless, every part of the balcony was wet. Right, I thought, so I'll have to go and drag out one of the fluffy rags from the non bathroom and roll around on it. I knew that this would do the trick as if I am at home and outside in the garden and it starts raining, Sheila rubs me down with my own little cat sized drying rag. I walked across the room, dripping all the way, into the non bathroom and I could see several of the white fluffy rags hanging above me. After a few leaps I managed to hook my claws onto one and then pull it down. So far so good. I managed to drag it back into the main room and then had a good rolling session on it - well that was all I could do for the moment. I went and had a drink and then sat down on the sofa still growling to myself. Suddenly this day I had been looking forward to so much had become a disaster day. Well, I suppose it could only get better. Eventually I nodded off.

I was awakened by Sheila coming in. Her smile of greeting was suddenly replaced by a look of horror when she saw me, my fur still damp and spiky, and the normally sparkling stateroom now not looking quite so sparkly! "What on earth has been going on here, Misty?" she gasped, then a look of realisation came over her face, "OMG, I forgot they were going to wash the windows this morning, I should have closed the doors to the outside!" She glanced around and then, for some unaccountable reason, just burst out laughing - that hyena like sound again! "I shouldn't laugh, Misty" she stuttered (no you damn well shouldn't!) "but I've NEVER seen you looking so scruffy" (well, thank you very much for that!) "and before I clean you and the room up, I must take a photo, nobody at home will believe the state you've got yourself in, everybody always says how pretty you are and how immaculate you keep yourself!!" (Well, dear, I'm "pretty" fed up now - the state I'VE got myself in? That's rich! You mean the state the WINDOW CLEANERS have got me in!) She picked up her phone and pointed it at me (that's right – humiliate me again when you show your friends at home!) By this time my fury was increasing by the minute. I have never, ever given Sheila a scratch, even when we have had the odd contretemps, but I certainly felt like giving her one now. However, sense prevailed and I thought I'd better not aggravate the situation any more so I merely wagged my tail and sat sulkily down in the corner. "Don't worry Misty" she soothed, "a nice blow dry will sort you out in a minute, and I must tidy up here or else Pedro will have a heart attack when he comes in later!

I watched as she fetched another of the fluffy white rags and carefully wiped down the walls where I had brushed against them, and also the sofa. She went outside and dried off the litter igloo and set the cushion out in the sun. I hoped it wouldn't take too long to dry as I wanted to catch the evening sun on it as I'd done before. Yes, I was getting into the pleasure of the cruising routine, dear reader, though this morning's events had somewhat marred today's experience! Opening a drawer she produced a hair dryer and picking up my brush and comb, sat me down on another drying rag and proceeded to dry my fur off and give me the promised blow dry. Aaah, this felt better. I always like being groomed. After a few minutes of blissful brush strokes accompanied by a nice warm rush of air, I felt my usual happy self returning and so began to purr. "Good girl, Misty" said Sheila, "All's well that ends well. Now you look gorgeous again and everyone will say how pretty you look. Pedro will not realise what a car crash this room looked like when I came in - though he may think I've used rather a lot of towels today – and all's well so we can get on with enjoying ourselves. I'll give you your lunch now and

I'll just have a quick wash and change and then we'll go up and have a nice coffee and then just have a leisurely afternoon because it's going to be a special night tonight being formal night!" Well, I certainly agree with all that I thought, and then enjoyed my lunch snack of cheesy crunchies while she sorted herself out and tidied away the bits of shopping she had bought when off the ship. I noticed another teddy had joined the gang. This one was wearing a vest with a strange name on it that began with the letter S and ended with the letter M. I suppose it was the name of the port where he had previously lived. He would find it different living in Cornwall! "Right, let's go" she said, so off we went.

Shortly we arrived at the frothy coffee lounge that Sheila loved, and she quickly settled herself into a comfy chair while I curled up under the table. Her friend Violetta came over, gave me a quick pat and brought over a large cup of the brown stuff. She stood chatting to Sheila for a while and then suddenly said "Ooops, look who's coming, I must get back to work!" She disappeared down to the end of the lounge where there was a counter with an array of tempting looking (to you humans who love sweet treats, not to we cats!) cakes and pastries. I wondered who was so important that she had to rush away and look busy! I peeped out and saw two of the crew members approaching, one was Pedro's boss, Tom, and the other was a tall dark haired man who had even more gold rings on his jacket than Tom had!

They stopped right by Sheila. Both of them gave her big smiles; she stood up and they all hugged each other. "Great to see you again, Dimitrios, Tom" she said. "I heard you were on board," the one she had called Dimitrios replied," and I will be seeing you at dinner tonight! It will be good to catch up on your news!" I listened. He spoke in a strange accent too ... not like Pedro's and definitely not Cornish! I wondered in just how many accents you humans speak! Cats basically miaow much the same except for our oriental cousins who do seem to have their own cat language! They continued to chat for a while, and then Dimitrios looked down at me and said "Well, well - who is this? I have met Truffles before (he grinned) but not you! Don't tell me you are writing a book too!" They all laughed and Sheila explained that, yes, I was doing a follow up to Truffles' book but it would be my own thoughts (possibly different from hers) about cruising on this beautiful ship. "Wonderful" said Dimitrios, "I look forward to reading it!" He bent down and gave me a pat. I moved forward and gave him one of my best pussy smiles plus a loud purr. "Now Misty", said Sheila, "you must be very well behaved because this is Dimitrios and he is the Master (or Captain as some people call him) of this ship! In other words, the really big boss or Top Cat to you!" They laughed again. Well, so he was Top Cat was he? I didn't know ships had masters - I thought it was only dogs that had masters. You learn something different every day don't you, and I sure was doing just that on this great adventure! I remembered that Sheila has mentioned the name Dimitrios before, she appears to have been friendly with him for several years, but I didn't realise he was the main man! "And this is Tom" she continued. "Ah, but Misty and I have already met" said Tom smiling and also giving me a pat. "You HAVE?" squeaked Sheila, "How on earth was that ...?" "Well I came round to your stateroom the other evening" he said, "just to check things as a matter of course due to health and safety regs because I knew you had a furry friend travelling with you" (more laughter) "Bimey" said Sheila, "Well I hope you found everything in order?" "Top marks!" replied Tom, "nothing to worry about. Everything was pristine, but I knew it would be anyway!" Thank goodness for that I thought. They chatted for a few more minutes and then with a final pat for me they left. Sheila sipped at her now rather cool coffee and I relaxed back under the table again and took a quick cat nap. It was nice to have met the Master, I reflected. I knew how he must feel being a master, or captain, because I am master (mistress) of our house too! So we had something in common! Some while later, Sheila nudged me awake and we returned to the stateroom.

I strolled outside and sat down in the sun which was still very bright. I could hear Sheila pulling drawers in and out and opening cupboard doors ... obviously the big decisions about what she was going to wear this evening were starting to be made. As I've said before, half her life seems to be taken up with deciding what clothes to array herself in! Eventually I heard the sound of music coming from the moving picture box and the clink of a glass. The afternoon canapés must have arrived, so time for me to go inside and see what treat was awaiting me! A couple of slivers of ham rolled around cheese and some turkey nibbles. Very acceptable. Oh yes, I could definitely get well used to this kind of life!

Back on my indoor bed, I decided to have a doze until my real dinner arrived. I knew she'd choose something nice. And yes it was ... creamed mackerel followed by little chunks of veal in a delicious sauce! Then Sheila, looking particularly sparkly this evening, departed for her own drinks and dinner with Dimitrios and friends saying she would collect me afterwards so we could go to the theatre and watch the spectacular show! Great stuff. I contentedly rolled over and fell into a doze again, only waking when Pedro arrived to accept another couple of shrimps! Full to the brim, I was a happy cat! I noticed that he'd made an extra special creature from the fluffy rags tonight (I believe it was that big bird you call a swan, though when I'd finished scratching its underside it maybe looked more like a floppy chicken) and also on the bed was a carry bag with the ship's name on it and some extra choccies.

A good while later Sheila arrived back, also looking happy. She was clutching a red rose and a large photograph. "Right, Misty", won't be a sec" she said disappearing into the non bathroom. A few minutes later out she came, put on my really expensive sparkly collar and lead (on me I mean, not her ... she's not that kind of human!) and off we went to the theatre. It seemed a long walk but eventually we arrived and sat where we'd sat before, her on one of the high seats at the back with me on the ledge in front. It wasn't long before the mewsic (sorry, music!) started and the show began. Right from the start it sounded very unique ... unusual magical sounding music and lots of people in really colourful and strange costumes singing and dancing to it. It almost felt tribal or as if everyone had gone back in time. All the people in the seats, including Sheila, were clapping and swaying to the rhythmic music, and I was too. Then Sheila nudged me "Look Misty, it's Peng Fei. Watch him, he's marvellous!" I peered down to see a figure throwing a shiny object up in the air and swinging it around - he seemed to be catching it on a piece of string! He carried on doing this for quite a while in all manner of ways. After much applause from the people watching and some more wonderful music and singing from the rest of the performers, he appeared again but this time seemed to be walking and swinging along on a piece of string himself! I was transfixed, I wasn't even sure a cat could balance like he could! Who exactly was Peng Fei? Mystery man? He could change his face at will, and now he was doing all this! No wonder Sheila has often said how nice it is to have him as one of her friends and proud she is of him! The show ended with a spectacular climax and everyone stood up and cheered in unison. "Well Misty" said Sheila, "that was great wasn't it? Now we'll go and see Peng Fei, he will be waiting outside the theatre to see people as they come out. He will be expecting me too!"

Following the slow moving mass of people leaving the theatre, we made our way down to the floor below and there she spotted Peng Fei waiting. When they had exchanged big hugs and greetings, I looked at him but up close he looked rather unusual, almost green with golden stripes on his face and, in fact, to me a bit scary! So I hid behind Sheila. "Well, Peng," I heard her say, "I think you've got more make up on than I have!" They both laughed. "Here's Misty" she said. "Hello Misty" said Peng Fei, "I've heard a lot about you" and he bent down to pat me, but I backed away, he did look a bit frightening! So many faces and now another one! "It's OK Misty" he said understandingly, "I can see I am looking strange to you, but I am made up like this for the show. I promise you

I am NOT scary and next time I see you I will look just like anybody else!" I looked up at Sheila and she was nodding in agreement, so I gingerly crept forward and let him pat me. Thankfully his hands looked normal! "You're a very pretty little cat" he said, "Sheila has sent me photos of you, but you look even better in real life!" Oh well, I thought, flattery will get you anywhere so on came the purr and from that moment we were buddies! They chatted for a while and arranged to meet up in a couple of days' time and we then went our separate ways.

Next stop was the noisy casino which seemed to be busier than ever tonight. However, somebody was already sitting at Sheila's favourite machine so we had to go to another one. "Come on Misty, bring me luck" she said, "sitting down in front of another. "Oh there's Val and Ken!" she exclaimed, and waved to a couple of people opposite who I recognised from the time we had played the game putting little balls into holes. "Brought your lucky cat with you?" chuckled Ken, "send her over here for a bit, I could do with some luck myself!" Sheila then proceeded to press her machine's buttons and hope that the right pictures came up. I did too, not necessarily for her sake but for mine so we could escape this noisy place! With a sigh I resigned myself to a long wait and tucked myself neatly under her seat. It did seem an age, but suddenly I heard a shout of delight coming from Val's direction swiftly followed by a squawk from Sheila! It seems both of them had won something from their machines as both had beaming smiles as they pressed their final buttons and got given the white slips of paper that seemed to please them so much. In their excited chatter following, all I could make out was that Val had made a profit of seventy dollars and Sheila a profit of fifty dollars. As I didn't know what a dollar was this didn't impress me! Ken didn't have such a big smile, though, as it appeared he had given his machine forty dollars! They talked a bit more and then they went off to find Dylan and we left on the bedtime trail, but stopping for Sheila's usual nightcap in the coffee lounge first. Back at the stateroom and ready for our respective beds, I reflected on my day. Apart from the disaster with the water early on (and fortunately Pedro never noticed anything amiss!) it had been a really good day so I went to sleep a contented little cat! Sheila, I'm sure, felt the same.

Life on board:

The following days of this lovely experience passed in a kind of happy blur. I was well and truly into the daily routine of living the high life on this beautiful ship, with everything I could ever desire (apart from one of those elusive white birds!) so close to paw. I began to understand why Sheila loves cruising so much when I compared it to the humdrum life we live at home. If there was perhaps the odd spider or butterfly to chase here and there, well I would rather like to live on a ship and if there was a vacancy going for a ship's cat, I'd be well up for it!

Most mornings Sheila would disappear and return about lunchtime with another of those wretched little bears to add to the motley collection that now stretched right along the back of the wall unit. I nipped up there one day and they, like the first two, were all wearing a tee shirt or jersey with the name of wherever they had come from ... strange names too, like Helsinki, Oslo, St. Petersburg, Tallinn and Warnemunde – the likes of which I'd never seen. Well, to be honest, apart from Cornwall, and now Southampton, I don't know the names of any places as my geography book only says back garden and front garden in it!

While she was away, I took full advantage of all the comforts of the stateroom and also Pedro's generosity with the tasty titbits he brought for me. He was well and truly under my thumb by this time! I did feel I was perhaps putting on a bit of weight, though it was nothing to the weight that was gradually piling onto Sheila, but who cares, we were both having fun, fun, fun! I heard her and some other people talking one day and it seems that most passengers (humans not cats!) put on about half a stone per cruise. I reckoned I'd put on about half a pound! As the weather continued warm and sunny, it was bliss in the mornings lazing on the balcony birdwatching and looking all around at each different port we stopped at - seeing so many strange buildings and lots of people moving around so far below me looking like ants. It made me feel quite superior, being on high like a queen looking down on her subjects! Fortunately I managed to avoid any more window washing disasters as, having learnt her lesson, Sheila made sure the outer doors were tightly closed whenever they came round again! I still enjoyed my scratching and clawing sessions on Pedro's animals each night, and somehow my luck held as neither he nor Sheila seemed to spot the odd little bits thread that dangled from their tummies afterwards!

One morning I noticed something of a disturbance happening below. Parked opposite us was a small and rather rusty looking cruise ship. I was idly watching passengers from both ships to-ing and fro-ing along the dockside between. An elderly lady was trying to come on board our ship, but as she arrived at the gangway and showed her pass, her arm was politely taken by one of the officials who pointed over at the other ship. It seemed she was a passenger on that ship, not ours! She retraced her steps but as soon as she reached ground level again, she turned around and back up the gangway she came!

The official pointed out the other ship once more! Back down she went only to return yet again! This performance happened twice more! By this time the official must have been getting a little impatient, but he kept his cool! Suddenly I saw Michael (my pal Mr Pumpkin) appear at the top of the gangway. The official must have explained what had happened so Michael then did his good deed for the day and gently drawing the old lady down the gangplank, he walked her over to the right ship. He told Sheila later that the old lady had told him that yes, she knew perfectly well that was her ship but she'd much, much prefer to come on our ship! Well, full marks for a good try dear!

In the afternoons we mostly went outside and walked around to the grass deck. Sheila would sit and chat to Dev, sipping one of his Pussyfoot specials, or to her friends Petra and Graham who often joined her there. I would enjoy a good roll around on the grass and then lie down and watch the people playing their ball games. Sheila had bought me my own little ball on a stretchy string from one of the shops below, so I enjoyed carrying it over to whoever was sitting nearby and putting on my hopeful expression - which never fails – and having them play my own games too! One day we were watching several passengers all prancing around and waving their arms to some loud music in what Sheila said was a Zumba class. She and Petra thought they'd join in too, so Graham took me over to the ice cream machine and we both enjoyed cooling down with this totally delicious stuff whilst the girls just got hot and sweaty! Ugh! What weird things you lot do for pleasure, you certainly wouldn't see me over exerting myself like that!

One afternoon Sheila took me to meet Peng Fei, her friend

that seems to be made of china! She told me she usually meets him for a meal one evening during her cruise in some specialised quirky eating place on board, and also for cups of their favourite frothy coffee at other times. She told me he wanted to meet me and show me some magic, so we'd go along and see him in the coffee lounge. Magic? What else does this made of china boy do I wondered – he changes his face, balances on bits of string and throws shiny objects about – and now magic too? Maybe he could magic me a little bird out of the sky! We strolled along to the coffee lounge and just as we were about to find a table, suddenly I heard somebody calling out "Hello Sheila" in yet another strange accent I'd never heard. Sheila walked over in the direction of the voice which was coming from the bar, dragging me behind, and said "Oh wow, Nestor, hi – how are you? Good to see you! I havn't been into Michael's Club yet so I wasn't sure you were on board!" (I didn't realise our Michael (Mr P) had a club as well - he seemed to do all sorts of jobs, maybe he was the ship's resident "dogsbody"! I know that's what you call people who seem to have lots of odd jobs to deal with. Needless to say, there are no 'catsbodies' – we cats wouldn't even consider overworking ourselves!) I looked up and saw yet another smiley man wearing those little round bits of glass in front of his eyes like Sheila does (I don't really know why you humans wear them, I've never seen cats wearing such things) But she must set great store by them as she wears them every day, and seems to have a drawer full of them in various colours. They chatted for a few minutes and then Sheila found a table, sat down and I took my usual observational position behind her ankles and we waited for Peng Fei to arrive.

Only a few minutes later he appeared … no, not by magic(!) he simply came walking towards us! Greetings exchanged he sat down, Violetta came and brought them their frothy drinks and they spent a few minutes sipping their drinks and chatting about this and that. "Well, Misty" said Peng Fei, leaning over and stroking my face, "I don't look too scary now do I?" Purr switched on, I thought no you look a very nice young man. "Well, Misty" he continued, "Sheila says you like playing ball games (yes I do, I do!) so I am going to show you a magic trick with some balls and cups. You must watch very carefully indeed and find the ball. Can you do that?" Of course I can, don't be daft! Why was Sheila grinning I wondered? He produced three cardboard cups (like the delicious ice cream comes in, though sadly they were empty) and stood them side by side on the ground in front of me. Then he showed me a nice little red ball. Ooh goody, is that for me? Peg Fei must have read my thoughts because he said "If you can find the ball under the cup, Misty, you can keep it! Now watch the ball, don't take your eye off it" My eyes are both stuck securely in my head, so how can my eye be on the ball … oh well, not to worry, just some other strange human expression I guess! I was really, really close to him now and he placed the ball under one of the cups and then quickly moved the cups around. But my eyes are very, very sharp and I was certain I could spot the ball under its cup with no problem. He stopped shifting the cups about and indicated that I should touch the cup which hid the ball. Easy … I tapped the middle cup! But ..… NO ball! I was watching his every move, I knew it was there! What the … "Oh dear, Misty" he smiled, "No, it's under HERE!" He tipped over the right-hand cup and sure enough there was the red ball! How on earth could I have missed that! Was I losing my touch? Sheila laughed, I scowled at her. "Come on Misty," said Peng Fei, "Let's try again!" Well, dear reader, he did the ball game another four or five times and I never found the ball once! I couldn't believe it ... how totally humiliating! "Well, Misty, " said Sheila, "I told you it was going to be magic. You can stay here all day but I'm afraid you'll never find the ball, Peng's too clever!" I had been looking forward to playing with that little red ball but now it seemed that wouldn't happen. I sat back defeated and switched on the pathetic look. But Peng Fei smiled and bounced the ball at me ... "Of course you can have the ball, Misty, I brought it specially for you anyway!" He picked me up and stroked me again. So all ended well. I'd made yet another new friend and I'd seen some close up magic where I simply could not believe my eyes, and I got the ball anyway! We sat there for a while, them talking and me sitting contentedly admiring my new toy!

On another afternoon instead of going outside, Sheila took me along the shopping street and after treating herself to some of the sickly sweet smelling disgusting stuff you like to spray yourselves with, she was just about to go into the ice cream place when she was hailed by Val and Ken who were also doing some shopping, judging by the number of bags they were carrying. (Maybe they'd won some more money in the casino!) "Come on Sheila" said Ken, "let's have a drink. We can sit outside the pub so it will be OK bringing Misty." Sheila nodded and so we turned away from the ice cream parlour. Oh dear, not a good plan I thought! But I couldn't do much about it could I?

We retraced our steps and arrived at the Dog and Badger where they all sat down around one of the tables outside. I retreated as far back under the table as I could. There was NO WAY I wanted to encounter a dog or, even worse, a badger! A barman came up and brought Sheila a glass of that pink stuff she likes, and Val's drink was more red in colour but the drink that Ken asked for really puzzled me as he asked for an Old Speckled Hen. What was this place, a flipping zoo? Dogs, badgers and now hens! And anyway, how can you 'drink' a hen, you chew it surely! And if there were hens around, wouldn't the dogs and badgers have eaten them? I shook myself, sometimes I think I must have an over-active imagination! Well, there was only one sensible solution, go into sleep mode ... so I did.

One evening we again joined up with Val, Ken and Dylan in the street as there was a grand parade of people all dressed up in fancy costumes and the singers and dancers from the theatre also joined in with lots of lively music. Everybody was enjoying themselves and dancing too! There were so many people that I felt in danger of being squashed under paw so in the end I jumped up on Sheila's shoulder where I had a better view anyway! Also on my perch I could do my own cat dancing to the music! Though later when we were back in the stateroom I felt a bit guilty when Sheila showed me the scratches I'd made on her shoulder! Several people took pictures of me on their little talking/picture machines which was good too! Fame at last, eh!

People do say funny things. On another afternoon we had been outside on deck with Sheila's friends Mary and Eric. Eric had gone off to play some ball games and Sheila and Mary decided to go to the spa and fur dressing section of the ship to book places on some kind of talk that was coming up called "Look ten years younger"! Don't kid yourself girls, waste of time, no chance! I would have preferred to stay outside on the lovely grass, but being attached to the lead gave me no option! Coming inside and arriving at the elevators, we could see another lady pacing up and down looking worried wringing her hands together and saying "How can I find them, where am I, oh dear I'll be late, what shall I do?" "Are you lost? Can I help you?" said Sheila, "I know this ship very well. Where do you want to get to?" The lady said that she wanted to get to the large observation lounge at the other end of the deck where people meet and can sit and view the sea, in the evenings have some naughty drinks and dance to music and so forth. She had to meet up with her family she added and had only about five minutes to get there. "Well, calm down ", said Sheila, "No problem. Just walk back along the deck and the entrance to the lounge will be right in front of you." "I can't possibly do that!" said the lady. "Why not?" asked Sheila. "I can't go on the deck because it's full of bodies!" she replied. Both Sheila and Mary did a double take! Bodies? There was a couple of stunned seconds silence ... then the penny dropped, she was referring to the rows of people sunbathing on the deck outside! But WHY couldn't she walk past them I wondered. I know that when you humans dress in fewer clothes than normal to sunbathe, some of you (particular the fatter ones ... sorry, miaow, miaow!) do look somewhat comical, but I wouldn't go so far as to say they look that frightening! "OK, OK" soothed Sheila, "well just get the elevator one floor down, then walk right along the passageway and get the elevator or walk up the stairs at the other end and you will find an inner entrance to the observation lounge." "Right" said the lady, calmer now, "Thanks" and she got into the elevator and disappeared. Sheila and Mary burst out laughing. "Well" gasped Mary "She'd better not come to Cornwall and go to the beach at Newquay then!"

After booking their (what a total waste of time!!!) places on the lecture, we strolled along the slightly lower deck to the large covered water pool where Sheila and Mary sat themselves down and ordered some cool drinks and an ice cream for me. I was glad we were sitting well away from all the water but near enough to the pool's end so that I could watch the coloured water spouts leaping up and down. "I'll tell you another funny story" said Sheila. "Go on then, "said Mary, I'm all agog!" "It wasn't on this ship" said Sheila, "but some years ago we were spending Christmas and New Year on a cruise. We were walking around the main foyer and a rather elderly lady came down the stairs towards us. We exchanged good mornings as you do, and then she looked at me and said "What day is it dear?" "It's New Year's Day" I replied. "Ah" she said, "and what day of the week is it dear?" "Er, um, it's Tuesday" I said. "And what ship am I on dear?" she said! Mary started laughing. Sheila said that when it got to the stage that if, let alone not knowing what day of the week it was, she couldn't even remember the name of the ship she was on, THAT would be the time she would give up cruising! She wouldn't want people like us looking at her and saying to each other look at that poor old soul doddering around! Well, dear, not all that many years to go I reckon (sorry Sheila, another miaow, miaow comment!) so yes, maybe the lecture on looking ten years younger might be of some use after all! I settled down to enjoy my ice cream while the others talked about the usual stories where some people, usually first time cruisers, say the daftest things like - Do the crew sleep on board? How does the electricity get to the ship and so on ...

Sheila said that many years ago when the cards that open cabin doors had only recently come into use, they were having a drink with a comedian they knew. He told them a true story where in one of his shows he had told his audience - purely as a joke - that the new cards were rather like bank cards, so maybe they should try them in a bank machine in the next port of call and see if they could get any money out! Believe it or not, apparently about seventy people DID actually try their cabin door cards in bank machines and, of course, lost them! The comedian was summoned to the office of the captain of the ship and given the telling off of his life! He had truly never assumed that people would really try to use their cards! Needless to say, he was ever invited back on that ship again!

I was really enjoying the routine of shipboard life and I know Sheila felt the same. She, of course, did a lot of stuff without me ... but with a lovely sunny balcony to lie on, titbits brought to me by Pedro, what more could I ask for! It was going to be back to earth with a real bump when we got home. I would have to instruct Sheila to wait on me more often!

The last three days were a rush of activity. We went to another of the fabulous ice shows, and another big song and dance show in the theatre and also to Peng Fei's unbelievable magic show. He made more than balls disappear I can tell you! One night we joined Sheila's friends June and Roger, and Petra and Graham, and we went to a smaller kind of theatre where there was a game called "Mr and Mrs" being played with three couples on stage. The host was asking them lots of questions and their answers seemed to throw the audience into hysterics! Talk about a bunch of laughing hyenas! What made them laugh the most was a question where the wives were asked if they knew the name of their husband's previous girlfriend. Two wives gave ladies' names but the third one just said "Bitch!" Personally I didn't see anything funny in that ... lady dogs are called bitches, I mean what's wrong with that? You humans love your dogs - almost as much as your cats - don't you? So I don't see why you would worry about being called a bitch! Again, there are just so many things I will just never get my head round when it comes to human behaviour and the strange things you think and say!

On the last afternoon Sheila took me with her to the final of some sort of question and answer game called "Progressive Trivia" that apparently was another activity that Mr Pumpkin (sorry, Michael) had been running throughout the cruise.. She hadn't been to any of the previous sessions but just came to watch the final and see which team won. She told me afterwards that she had written some quiz books (about cats and dogs) and Michael had said he was going to use some of her questions in this final. I found it all rather boring really and dozed off and on at her feet. However, one question did catch my ear! It was about cats! "What do you call a group of cats?" And nobody knew the answer. I couldn't believe it! Do you, dear reader? No? Well, a group of cats is called a clowder!

After getting up early and packing her cases, also during the last day Sheila had dragged me around saying goodbye to all her friends on board, both those who worked on the ship and those who were guests. They had all been such nice friendly people, and I felt glad to have met them and seen another side of Sheila's world. Now I could understand even better how she loves to get herself away two or three times a year from her rather isolated life at home in Cornwall. And I have to say it makes a break for me too when I go off to the local cat camp!

My last delicious dinner was a prawn in a cheesy sauce starter followed by duck bits in gravy and to finish, a little pot of ice cream into which Pedro had stirred a drop of fish oil! How thoughtful of him, and how very yummy! I gave him an extra special purr and ankle rub and as he picked me up and gave me some nice strokes and pats, I think I might have caught a tear in his eye. Aaah! Sheila had given him, on my behalf, a big box of those chocolate things that you humans like, so I hoped that when he ate them he would remember his first, and probably last, cat guest!

After Sheila returned from the last show of the cruise, she heaved her cases outside the stateroom door, all appearing to be much heavier than when she'd arrived! Well, I could have saved her some of the weight by chucking those pesky little teddy bears overboard, couldn't I? But that, I fear, would have been more than my life's worth! Our house is already overrun with stupid teddy bears - I guess I would have to put up with another seven pairs of eyes looking at me!

We had a final visit to the coffee lounge where Sheila enjoyed her last frothy coffee and Amoretto drink, whilst I enjoyed strokes and pats from the other people there and posed for lots of pictures! Well, I do like being the centre of attraction, so why not milk it! Though I was showing everybody my best happy pussy face, in fact, all the people, including Sheila, looked rather gloomy and they were all saying they didn't want the cruise to end! Back at the stateroom for our last sleep, it did make me feel sad that we were leaving, but I was also just happy to have had the experience ... and I would enjoy boasting about it all to the neighbouring cats at home!

Going home:

Morning came and Sheila woke me up at a much earlier hour than I was accustomed to, and she rushed around giving me rather a scrappy breakfast and hustling me outside to do my morning washing and toilet procedures. Alright, alright - keep your hair on I thought grumpily to myself, what's all the rush. But after emptying and cleaning the litter igloo, she had disappeared and so I spent the next twenty minutes or so grumbling to myself and looking through the glass doors at the hardly welcoming sight of Southampton docks in the rain with not even a cushion to sit on as all my stuff had been packed. When she returned, she clipped on the lead (well, at least I won't have to wear that again I thought) and we made our final journey to the elevator where there were lots and lots of people already waiting. We'll be stuck here for ages, I thought gloomily, and so we were ... but thankfully we did get into an elevator eventually. I looked around as always trying to spot the lady who announced the deck numbers, but no I never found her. It will remain one of life's unsolved mysteries to me.

Arriving at the lower deck we joined another long line of people, not nearly so cheery now as when they got on the ship I noticed. Maybe they all wanted to stay on too. A thought crossed my mind that if I escaped from the lead I was sure I could run off and hide somewhere and then maybe we could stay on board and do the whole thing all over again! While

Sheila was talking to someone I tugged at the lead and, yes, I nearly made it as I felt her grip loosen but "Oh no you don't Misty" she said and so that was my plan well and truly scuppered.

Getting off the ship didn't take nearly so long as getting on, we merely walked off with Sheila inserting her card into the same little machine that had squeaked when we arrived reminding me that there was probably a family of mice living in there! There was quite a long trek down the sloping zig-zagging passageway before we arrived in a huge - and scarily noisy to me - space filled with thousands of cases like Sheila's. How on earth was she going to spot hers amongst all that lot I wondered, quickly pressing myself into her leg as a man trundling a big trolley passed rather too near for comfort. That was close, I nearly did get flattened then! Sheila looked down and got the message. She picked me up and and called to another man nearby with a similar trolley. We followed him to the mass of cases but near to I could see that they were actually stacked in neat rows and it didn't take long before Sheila found all of ours. I was glad of that. I had no wish to never see my bed, collars and comfy cushion again! The man stacked them on his trolley (I'd have rather liked a ride on his trolley too!) and then walking out of the building, there was Tony waiting for us with the motor machine, as shiny as ever. The man gave the cases to Tony, who groaned at the weight of them. "Every time you come home with nearly double what you bring!" he said to Sheila, who just grinned at him. "Well, you ought to know me by now Tony!" she said. Then, somehow after fitting it all into the motor machine, there was just about room for us so we got ourselves in, I curled up on Sheila's lap and off we went … Cornwall here we come again!

So, what a treat I'd had … and I've something to tell all you folks too! If you've never been on a cruise before, well get off your backsides and GO on one! You will enjoy!

ABOUT THE AUTHOR

Sheila Collins was born and brought up in Croydon. She attended Selhurst Grammar School and then went on to Croydon Technical College where she completed a one year secretarial course. During the years that followed Sheila held various secretarial/PA posts at managerial and directorial levels in London, Bournemouth and, latterly, in Cornwall, where she lives now. In recent years she has channelled her word power into the successful humour of the Truffles' Diaries series of books and both Truffles' and now Misty's adventures at sea. Being a lover of dogs as well as cats, she has also produced several other pet orientated books. Sheila holds a diploma in illustration and cartooning, a skill she puts to good use, though in Misty's books there are no actual illustrations, just a charming picture of her (Misty, not Sheila!) on the front cover. This is Sheila's ninth published book from Apex Publishing. She lists her pleasures in life as the 'Three C's'... cats, cruising and chocolate – in no particular order.

www.ingramcontent.com/pod-product-compliance
Lightning Source LLC
Chambersburg PA
CBHW022037170626
46808CB00003B/1242